UNDER SNOW

LY DE ANGELES

&

SERENITY DE ANGELES

UNDER SNOW

LY DE ANGELES & SERENITY DE ANGELES

ISBN 9780648502593

Revised Edition, 2024

Cover design DÙTHCHAS PRESS

To the Romany Gypsies the greatest curse you can aim at someone is isolation. To be bereft of your ancestors, squabbling brothers, inspirations and livestock is to be only just alive.

Dr. Martin Shaw, *A Branch of the Lightning Tree*

.

All the birds of the air

fell a-sighing and a-sobbing,

when they heard the bell toll

for poor Cock Robin

Tommy Thumb's Pretty Song Book, 1744

The most beautiful thing we can experience is the mysterious. It is the source of all true art and science.

Albert Einstein

Lord, what fools these mortals be!

William Shakespeare,

Midsummer Night's Dream, Act 1 Scene 1

Go n-éirí an bóthar leat…

(May you succeed on the road)

Irish blessing

We call them faerie. We don't believe in them. Our loss.

Charles de Lint

YOU REALLY SHOULD BELIEVE IN FAERIES, warns Sheldrú. *Not the painted, winged kind but the real ones. The kind you'd pass on the street and not recognize because they look like nobody you want to ever know.*

You really, really should believe in faeries. Because if you make the mistake of looking into their eyes, thinking they're just another person, it'll be too late. All of a sudden life is never the same again.

Trust me. I never lie.

PART 1

1

64 LAFAYETTE STREET

WHAT A STREET IS LAFAYETTE? A FEW boarded-up concrete and dirty brick or weathered cinderblock buildings covered in tag. Every shop, open or long gone out of business but unable to sell since the economy went to shit back in oh-eight, is barred at both windows and doors. The alleys between buildings reek of old booze and piss, some of death, and all of garbage not picked up by the city in god knows how long.

A take-away kebab joint and a Sizzlers burger place miasma their grease-smell out into the midday, knowing no one'll come by until after four, and behind the counter of the 7-Eleven, selling fags and porn magazines, the poor young guy in the silly uniform, scrolls through a phone for his music, wishing he was anywhere but here. A two-dollar shop that's probably a front for money laundering, spreads its wares onto the pavement, and a cafe awakens, the manager filling the chalkboard with the specials at lunchtime. That'll see a mediocre but appreciative trade when the steelwork's upper management clock off at midday. They'll be by for gluten free salads and soy lattes.

Anyone in this neighborhood will do anything necessary to pay the rent.

Junked cars up on bricks, one rundown clapboard house after the other. A place where nobody can afford to care. Any gardens to speak of long gone to seed and cooch grass.

The wonder is, though, there's a living tree in that street. Just the one: sixty foot high and proud as you please. 64 Lafayette, Rathmore West, Rathmore County is the address of Ailín and Rose Wen, father and daughter, and home to a hundred-year-old rowan tree, an adult when the suburb was still a forest, that some visionary or long-dead architect decided to leave living. In leaf-bud now, above the roof of this house that hasn't been painted in years with its tiny front yard, weedy and refuse-strewn. Wire-link fence. Cast-iron gate still swinging open in the middle of summer for its own reasons but mostly rusted to the pavement, frozen in place in winter.

Around the back of the house, that proud tree shades a fence made of corrugated-iron, a tiny tool shed, a bit of a wooden bench and a cracked, weed-hopeful concrete path. The garden is a riot of food-bearing plants, herbs and flowers, especially flowers. Roses mostly.

The trunk of the rowan is like a woman in the olden days trying to fit herself into a girdle or a corset, wedged in the corner where the house and the fence meet, holding her breath and trying not to attract attention.

Inside is sad and drab. Raggedy and threadbare. Furniture used by somebody else once upon a time that is neat and clean for all that it's seen better days.

Rose Wen is Ailín and Orla Wen's daughter. Róisín Séala's granddaughter. She'll be twenty on her birthday come next winter. On the first day of December. Wild red hair, the color of new pennies, unlike anyone else in her family. Severely restrained by a hair tie. No makeup obscures the constellation of small freckles on skin that never tans. Deep, mossy green, unhappy eyes, a body as lean as a boy, and she is curled, cat-like on the couch in a position that should be impossible but isn't. Her forehead's scrunched in concentration as she reads, back and forth between one of the texts from a stack she's borrowed from the college library, her laptop and her handwritten notes in that big old black-covered art book that she carries around with her most places, in defiance of technology, as a diary more than for anything else.

Her father knows better than to have the sound up on the television when Rose is studying so he watches the screen pretending to read lips. He's forty-five but he stopped counting birthdays when his love died. He's as Irish as guilt and poetry, with dark, shaggy, shoulder-length hair shot through with the silver of grief, bright brown eyes that miss nothing despite the booze, his haggard, handsome face needing a shave. His attempt at seeming happy, for Rose's sake, constant hard work for usually no gain. An old habit.

He sits in his lazy-boy chair in front of the television, the volume on mute, dressed in worn down denims, a once-white thermal undershirt, a thick waistcoat and his plaid woolen dressing gown. He's got a quarter-full glass of whiskey in his hand and though he seems trapped in that little square of colored pixels, most of the time he isn't really watching anything outside himself at all. But not this time. His eyes widen and he sits upright.

'Róisín, can you look? It's the news about the tempest the weather people are calling *Eleanor*. Can you look, Róisín? She's smashing the west coast. Can I turn up the sound?' Rose ignores him so he does. Just a little, leaning forward in his chair.

'Hundred kilometer an hour winds, Róisín, and the power's out. Be cursed by all the spirit of the land the Blackwater looks to flood. If it washes your mother's remains away there'll be the devil to pay the púka.'

Rose looks up from her homework for just a second before, uninterested, she returns to her books. It's just another storm, thousands of miles away in a country she doesn't even remember.

'Róisín, *a cara*. Talking of the devil I've got a true story about when our man Gyofan went up against the Fair Folk.' He laughs from deep inside, his eyes watery but animated for the first time in days. Or is it years?

'Fair Folk, indeed, they say. There's never been a reason, outside of their presence, to call them that. She looked like an old woman. I tell you true as night follows day she nearly trapped him. It was a winter as cold as the one we just lived through. At a camp down by that very same

Blackwater River, just up the road from Cork and down from Galway. Do you remember? While everyone else was sleeping he's cursed with being wide awake, thinking on his mam and all the babies he'd seen born in the company of your own *seanmháthair*, bless her immortal self, while he's sitting up alone by the fire—'

'Daidí, please shut up. I can't study.' She moves her pile to one side of the couch uncurls and strides to the bathroom, shutting the door. He can hear her peeing. His beautiful, forest-eyed daughter. The flush sounds, the tap runs above the sink and the door opens, her still drying her hands, dropping the towel onto the back of the couch as she resumes her vigil.

'I should be quiet now, then, shouldn't I?' He looks at her. The stoniness of her lips. The pretense of noncommittal apathy that's really anger, as though he isn't even there. He knows she stopped listening long ago.

Ailín, sighs and turns off the television. 'That Emmet man phoned here again, did I tell you?'

'He's an idiot, he's disgusting, and he's as old as you are,' she mumbles, not looking up from her books.

'Don't you worry about him then, *a cara*. There'll be somebody important for you. I can feel it in my waters, and you know I'm never wrong.'

Rose pierces him with a dart of a look he doesn't care to interpret. He won't even try anymore.

He slides on his old shoes, and stands carefully, hanging onto the arm of the chair, smiling and tipping his head to the side like everything's alright. He downs the dregs of his glass and leaves the room, only to come back pulling on his big old all-weather coat and his tweed cap.

He pockets his cigarettes and pats at the jacket and pants with concern. 'I'll be going out for a while.'

She doesn't so much as blink. But Ailín's look is remorseful and embarrassed. 'Right then.'

'What is it, Dad?'

'Róisín. Sorry, I am again, but could you lend a man a bit of cash?' She opens her purse and hands him a tenner.

'I get my cheque on Thursday.' He shuffles to the small table for his Zippo and house keys, his brow furrowed with little frown lines like hillocks and hollows on a moor. 'I'll be home by midnight, like always.'

He kisses her cheek and staggers a little. 'And I'll fix you up for the other times I owe as well, so.'

He opens and closes the front door with a silence that defies the decrepitude of the patched up excuse at security. Rose's eyes well up. She wipes at them with her sleeve and returns to her work.

The back yard is all shadows and hints, in the light of the cloud-scuddy moon. Frosty night, as only early spring can be. The púca, a faerie man, understands his quest. Robin Kipling is the name he's known by. Not a mortal, but who has the look of being so, seeming to be in his early twenties, although appearances are deceiving. He's made himself comfortable between two branches of the rowan, just slightly higher up than the rusted bit of aluminum awning over the kitchen window.

He's fine looking, face pale in the streetlight, wind-chapped cheeks, deep brown eyes and raggedy hair the color of a dark horse, wearing worn denim jeans, and a T-shirt under a plain brown woven wool waistcoat, with a tarnished silver fob chain attached to something unseen in the pocket. Jacketless despite the bitter cold. A flattened-out, once-black old top hat is pulled low to his ears, from each of which glint thick gold rings.

He smiles. It'd light the dreams of anyone, man or woman. He shimmers, a mirage on the horizon of a desert highway, and disappears.

...

2

HOW LONG'S A PIECE OF STRING?

BUT... SAYS SHELDRÚ, *before I tell of what happens on that fateful night I need to backtrack, just a little, or I'll get you very lost. How, otherwise, to trust me?*

West Rathmore Senior High School is a bus ride away from 64 Lafayette Street, and no matter what the weather it's the only way Rose can get there and home again every day of the week. Reminiscent of a nineteenth century, convict-labor-built brick prison, but with temporary ugly duckling classrooms clustered around a mother that couldn't give a shit, it's gloomy all year. Sun, rain, fog, or snow as thick as a wolf pelt in an arctic blizzard.

The main three story building hasn't seen council funding in eleven years or more, and a thin coating of slag—or fallout from acid rain—from the steelworks upwind, clings to its surface, eroding history as well as the facade. Can hit the lungs, too, that air, if a person lives to be old enough, those who haven't smoked or drunk themselves to death before fifty. But there's been enough money raised by the parent body to get weapon screening at the entrances and exits, and a heavily-armed, private security presence to police inside and out.

Today's bright and blustery despite no heat from the sun, and the elms that line the perimeter of the asphalt quadrangle are in early leaf bud, just like the rowan, informing that winter is truly gone.

Rose sits bent over exam papers at one of the tables in the staff canteen. She's with her supervisor Sam Black-Squirrel, an indigenous man somewhere in his middle twenties, with black hair and eyes, a flat face with a strong jaw. He's busy marking the essays of students having difficulty writing by hand, unable to spell. Rose is trying to see what he does. To read them impartially. To understand how good some of them are.

Jimmy Wong comes in just ahead of Emmet Neam who occasionally phones Rose's home phone, though how he got the number he's not telling and she refuses to be trapped into asking. He should know better but she's worked out he's a creep. She's certain he's harmless or he'd have made a move by now. He's dressed in the gear of an athlete that just makes him sadder-looking, his shape that of somebody who eats too many burgers and too much take-away pizza and drinks way too much beer.

Jimmy's a different kind of person, a music teacher in love with

Coltrane and Led Zeppelin, Mozart and Pussy Riot. Always ready with a smile and never known to badmouth anyone. He's attractive to many of the staff members because of it. He's single, lives alone and wafts charm and good manners, asking opinions on art and sixties vinyl. Not really caring what anyone thinks and seemingly unconscious of attempts at seduction. He gets a coffee from the espresso machine and adds creamer before noticing his friends.

'Hey Sam, hey Rose.'

They acknowledge him as he settles his earbuds into his ears, cueing music on his phone.

Rose's smile in response stays on her face even as she dismisses him. She doesn't miss the look from Sam's guileless, hooded eyes, returning her attention to the papers. Her throat flushes pink.

'Books and extreme sports, Rose. Vérité?' Sam suggests.

'What?' Like she doesn't know.

'Creative processes and near-death experiences. Better than relationships.'

The flush spreads to her cheeks.

'You fancy him,' Sam blurts, tactlessly.

'Can we not talk about this?'

He sighs theatrically. 'One day the woman I'll be able to love will come right out of the pages of my novel. Maybe then I'll change my mind.'

'You got a *yes*?'

'Galleys in the mail next month.'

'What did you mean?' Rose persists.

'You're being obscure, Ms. Wen.'

'About relationships?'

'They're fucked,' Sam says, like it's just a statement and everybody probably knows except her. 'Haven't met a human could come close to matching my muse.'

'You're too fussy.'

'No. I'm honest. Besides, he's not your type.'

'Oh, so now I have a type?'

Sam checks his watch. 'Got to run.'

He sorts through the essays and hands her two he's marked with A's. 'Work out why these scored so high.'

'Thanks, I think,' she frowns. She's reading when Emmet sits beside her in the chair just vacated by Sam, a can of Coke dripping condensation down his hand, glancing at the pile and snorting back a laugh.

Rose rubs her eyes, irritated, and glances at him through her fingers.

'So Rosie—' he studies her, wondering why she never looks him in the face. 'Students torn you apart yet?' He's about to put the can intentionally onto the student papers. She moves them just in time.

Emmet is oblivious and picks up an essay at random, reading the childishly hand-written title before waving the page about as if to emphasize his point.

'Cat shit in a shoebox, Rosie—'

'Rose.'

'You really think these kids give a tuppenny fuck about this when they got dick rap to try on for their two minutes of Instagram fame and a future on social security payments to look forward to?'

Rose tries to snatch it from him, but he avoids her grasp. 'This

Shakespeare? Once you're a proper teacher you'll come to realize just how much time you're wasting. Just do what you have to and go home.'

Rose snatches back the essay. 'If you never bother how do you know?'

It's as though he doesn't hear or doesn't really care what she says. 'Sweetness, these kids is like one of them fucking riddles that don't have an answer. You know, like how long's a piece of string? You'll just end up middle aged and bitter.'

Jimmy overhears the conversation, his lips twitching at Emmet's stupidity.

'Twice as long as half its length,' she replies. Jimmy mouths the answer, smiling and tilting his head without looking up, not trusting that he can keep from laughing aloud.

'Pardon?' Emmet, offended, doesn't understand why.

'That's the answer,' she says, her voice arsenic.

Emmet snorts. 'Rosie, come for a drink this weekend?'

She pushes her chair back, picks up the essays and her laptop, and walks towards the corridor on the other side of the open door.

'Dinner maybe,' he calls after her. 'I'll bring the riddles and the pizza and the beer. You can thank me in your own time. We'll just see if you really do have all the answers.'

Rose closes the door behind her, and Jimmy leans towards Emmet.

'You hitting on her? Really?'

Emmet leans back and stretches. 'Ah Jimmy, me young chink son, she's playing the game. Chicks do that all the time.'

'The game?' says Jimmy Wong, knowing exactly what Emmet means.

'This little *catch-me-if-you-can* thing.'

'You think?'

'I'm the master of the fucking game. I don't think, I know.'

Jimmy turns up the volume on his music, wishing he was anywhere else.

...

3

DEATH BY FORTUNE

IN THE SMALL, ONCE LOVELY, NOW shoddy and stale, booze-smelling Sailor's Rest Hotel, Ailín sits on a barstool in the company a half dozen other men, all a bit drunk, and all used to the booze, a way of life with nowhere to go, no real homes. Forgotten men. Something dead in all of them except for coming here and doing this, remembering who they once were, the dreams of love and being significant in the world. Before the roadside bomb that one of them had joked about before it took out six of his friends, that stupid bravado that'll haunt him till he takes one too many pain-killers. The nightmares of another. The tragedy of not belonging anymore. Before the redundancy or the bigotry, before the kids left home and he turned too ugly to love. Before this, anyway.

Even if they're still young, they're old. Except Robin, taking up a stool. Robin, a stranger to all of them except Billy Shando, many years older than Ailín Wen, a shock of wiry grey hair, bright grey eyes, the worse for wear because of the drink—in junk shop, hand-me-down sweatpants, several jumpers and sneakers that should not be worn in the left-over snow, still clinging to the dark places like hope amidst helplessness.

Out of the corners of their minds they momentarily consider Robin. An interloper? Maybe. Maybe not. Him smiling a bit too much, a man not appearing old enough to hang with this lot, but hey, he's drinking along, and Ailín—an Irish gypsy who wishes for all the world he could forget it—is watching the younger man like he's a long lost son, or something to make a horse shy perhaps. He knows what he is even though he's not met the likes of him in this life, or even the one he ran away from.

Only Billy Shando understands just what it is that Ailín sees. That Ailín knows who and what Robin is, and why he's here tonight. The portend. An omen. Only Billy Shando truly knew his mother, Róisín Séala, whose destiny it was to deliver children, Ailín the only child of her own. To tell fortunes, leave a gift to her dear, sad granddaughter, and die otherwise unremembered.

'—and Gyofan is sitting by the fire deep in the poetry of some song,' continues Ailín, 'when that seeming old woman joins him. She pours whisky into a tin cup from the flask in her carry bag and holds it out to him. As you know, however, a clever man has to be careful because if she's of the Fair Folk he's dead if he doesn't know the rules. So Gyof is in a state of confusion because he knows he's right. He's bothered she'll best him, see? Just like I don't know how many times, or so the story goes. But you don't let them do you a good deed, that's the one thing he remembers learning at his grandmother's knee.

'So he stands from his seat by the fire, scared a bit shitless but not wanting her to guess and he knocks the cup away as though it's an accident.' He gestures wildly, his drink splashing. 'He says, *Oh, bejesus, I'm sorry! Can I make you a cup of tea instead?*'

The three sheets to the wind audience of half a dozen old blokes remember how this goes. There's a few knowing nods of *yeah, you got to keep them fooled till the sun comes up and they turn back into mists and forests and hares and owls and suchlike*, but they applaud, true to form, and the publican pours him a dram on the house so Ailín's a happy man.

Towards eleven, supposed to be coming on closing time, except who's checking so the publican doesn't really mind. Other than the lads with the Irishman there's only a few patrons remaining in the bar with the exception of the strangers. Seven of them. Men. Shadowed around the eyes. Jittery. Including Thomas Brody Reed, a shaved-headed younger man who's seen the inside of a prison more than once, for smashing up a phone booth and selling pot. Getting caught at it. Not violent but one who puts out that he can take care of himself.

And the other. The one in charge. Dressed all in black like he's in mourning. Like he belongs in a better part of town and is slumming, with a bespoke haircut, danger in his eyes, *Ray Bans* holding back stray locks from his forehead. Good bones but soft features on a face with a sensuous mouth. He could be an actor, or a musician in a band with that bright bluebird tattooed on the back of one hand, a broken chalice on the other.

He turns casually in his chair, the better to concentrate on Ailín, his smile not reaching those pale, unreadable eyes.

'And all that was left was his gloves and his pig. What do you think of that then?' Ailín finishes the story and his friends rowdy-up in tears of laughter.

'You're a stupid motherfucker is what you are.' Quiet, but not so everybody doesn't hear. 'You need to go back where you came from, old man.'

Ailín's friends, not including Billy Shando, watch the stranger, uncomprehending, their jaws hanging open and him laughing because of it. A sound like metal wheels on gravel.

'You need to shut your mouths, lads,' the stranger says softly, dangerously. 'The flies'll lay their maggots in them, just like your mothers got with you, you're not careful.'

Ailín is drunk or he'd know better, despite him recognizing Robin for what he is. He staggers to his feet as Billy turns white, recognition in his eyes, his lips one thin and bloodless line. 'Old man, is it? I could fight you all with one hand behind my back, punk.'

Robin drags him by the sleeve of his coat saying, 'Don't.' An order.

Ailín brushes the grip away, scowling but reclaiming his seat. This is not a brawler pub and the barman calls it a night earlier than he'd intended. The last thing he needs is the cops getting interested in the Sailor's being open after eleven.

'Right lads, ten minutes to closing. Last round.'

The man at the table downs his tequila shot glass, no lemon, no salt, drops his dark glasses over his eyes, making himself peculiarly forgettable, pushes back his chair and walks for the exit followed by the others in his pack.

The impotent old men mumble final orders to the barman. Except Billy Shando who's had enough for one night.

Ailín sidelines Robin, whispering, 'Is the rainbow's end empty now, so?'

'You drained the coffer dry, Ailín,' Robin says softly so no one else can hear. 'I'm here to set things to rights, because your time is done, me old son.'

Ailín sighs, resigned but not sad, as Robin dismisses him, seeming to trip over nothing, pretending to be drunk when he never can be. He gives Billy Shando a tip of his hat and a look of subtle warning, before turning his attention to the other men, his mess of unruly dark hair spiking in all directions. He bows theatrically, and clears his throat, his eyes trapping Ailín.

'I've got one,' he says, his accent as thick as any tinker.

Ailín changes his attitude to one of fun and his fellow drinkers laugh. 'Now your showing off!'

'A story, is it?'

'Can you match Alan here?'

'Wouldn't even try, but it's a true story.'

'Go on. Entertain us, then.'

Robin shoves the hat back on his head. 'Has anyone here heard of a haunted place called Castle Pook?'

'Bejesus I been there,' says Ailín.

'You're joking!'

'I am not. We used to travel the old roads once.'

'You're Pavee?'

'What?' The barman, like most of the others, has never heard the word before.

'Travelers. Like gypsies,' Robin adds, pinking at the cheeks, as though he could possibly feel embarrassment. Doing it for Ailín.

'Grand days before the government men took us out. The vardos of bright colors and horses walking slow in the traces. We used to camp under the stars, the nights alive with music. Well anyway it all went to shite. Cars now, and dirty big blocks of council flats.' He returns to the present and the gathering around him. 'So what's this story then?'

'In the time of the first queen Elizabeth—' Both he and Ailín spit on the floor. 'The silly-looking bald old hen was giving out great tracts of land in our west, down along the coast that looked across the sea to Tír na n'Óg.' Robin shimmers out of focus and Ailín, engrossed, is momentarily taken aback. He dismisses it, knowing what this is all about and being prepared to play along.

'So she gives a big chunk of Irish land to her two pretty fellers, Spencer and Walter Raleigh where legend has it—' He puts his finger to the side of his nose in an ancient gesture, 'that on the night of Midsummer the *daoine maithe*—the Fair Folk—have themselves a grand ball. And may any god around at the time help the mortal who just happens to be passing.'

'And the Fair Folk are?' asks the publican.

'What fuckwits erroneously call faeries,' Robin says quietly, a glint of danger in his eyes.

Ailín comes close to the other man's ear and whispers, 'You look after my girl, your lordship. Promise me that.'

'Goes without saying. But I do. I promise, As the land is my mother.'

A clock somewhere in the city chimes twelve bells, Ailín, alone in the dark and overcast night, smiles as he steadies himself against the closed door of the pub and pulls his coat tighter against the cold. He shambles off down the deserted street but as he passes a particularly shadowed alley, the pack from that table in the pub appear from the dark where they've been waiting.

The man with the bluebird tattoo leans languidly against a boarded-up storefront while Thomas Reed chest-butts Ailín, a forced smile turning up the corners of the mouth in an otherwise bewildered, bothered face.

Ailín punches out, wildly but ineffectually, and all of them, except the bluebird man, lay into him with fists and boots, swearing and jeering, the bashing mercilessly. Ailín laughing and crying.

They beat him unconscious before dragging him into the alley and dumping him on a pile of garbage bags beside an overfull dumpster.

The bluebird tattooed man pulls a black licorice-papered cigarette from a tarnished silver case and light it, blowing blue smoke into the frosty night, before following after his men as they stride off into the unseen.

At 64 Lafayette Street Rose is asleep on the couch, her paperwork dropped to the floor, dreaming again of the event that changed her life.

I'm five or six, and I have hold of Orla's hand. Orla is my mother. A beauty with creamy, freckled skin. Hair black, in flyaway braids to her waist. What color are her eyes? That's part of the dream I never remember. And it haunts me. Her clothing is brightly colored with, flowers of the field and she's like some queen in beads and bangles and earrings, her cleavage unapologetic, her feet in sturdy boots, covered with the dust of the road. No socks. Fine hairs below the knees. We've walked all the way from the camp on that field close to the old tower ruins a few miles away and the rain has held off. Rare warmth to the day. We're with two other women, and when we enter the little grocery store a bell over the door tinkles. They each take up one of the plastic carry baskets.

Inside are two pasty, mean-lipped village wives, both in overcoats. The one in pink fake fur has had her hair bleached to Nordic blonde. The shopkeeper, Arthur Dowd, wears a leather apron as he restocks shelves behind the counter. He appears as though he'd be more at home butchering something he'd recently killed than weighing flour, and he has his eyes fixed on us. The woman in the pink coat leaves, saying 'Make the call, Arthur. I'll see if Michael's still about.'

The barrel man crosses both his arms and places them on the bench, a barrier, his eyes on my mother.

'I don't serve tinkers,' he says, grinning through a mouth of missing teeth, 'unless you want to come out back with me.'

Except for Orla, the Travelers ignore him, dropping groceries into their baskets.

'We've got money,' she says, answering back at him, her head high.

An old dial-up phone is attached to the wall and he picks up the handset, punching the numbers on the keypad, malice in every stabby punch. He waits and we do nothing.

'Mam?' I'm scared again. I feel it all through me, like every time I dream this same dream.

'Shh,' she hushes me. 'It'll be alright, I promise.' She squeezes my hand and smiles and I believe her. God help me, I always believe her.

'Arthur Dowd from the village. The grocers, that's right. Yes, that's right. No, it's tinkers.'

'What're you doing calling the Garda?' She is smiling. Not wanting him to see her fear. Not giving him the satisfaction.

'Right. Thanks,' he says into the mouthpiece, ignoring her, hanging up, wiping his hands on his apron as though he's touched something dirty. 'They're coming in from town now, so either you go, or you're to deal with them instead.'

'I told you, we got money.' Orla replies, sure now of the pointlessness of anything she might say.

The women who came with us have put the tins and butter and flour and cabbages back on the shelves and stowed the baskets near the entrance again.

Arthur Dowd turns his back, reaching for the heavy broom in the corner and I'm hiding behind my mother as he comes at us, wielding the sweeper like a weapon.

'Get the feck out of my establishment,' he spits, coming at Orla. One of the Traveler women with us clutches her sleeve, dragging her out the door to the sound of that stupid, tinkling, manic little bell.

We're on the footpath, and the rain is torrential, making the cobbles, and the weeds, and all the other shops blur out of focus. Then the biddie in the pink jacket who left earlier arrives with two big cocky men.

One of them, in coveralls with a dark blue raincoat flapping uselessly says 'Where's the rest of them, then?'

'I'll curse you,' Orla yells over the loudness of the squall, not quite as sure of herself as she makes out, determined to protect me, as well as the others, crowding behind her, wanting to be gone.

'You're a dirty shraoilleog, is what you are, says the shorter of the two, 'with the filthy wee child, poor thing that she is too. And, by the holy mother of god, who'd you have ta fuck to make a brigid like her, then?'

Orla slaps his face and he hits her back with his closed fist. Her look is one of questioning as she falls. Her head hits the concrete with a surprisingly loud cracking sound. Blood pools all around her head and drags her unraveled night-black braids into the gutter along with it, the rain sending it flushing in all directions. Her eyes are open but the life is gone. Looking at eternity. Something meant behind the terror. Something I don't understand. Me trapped in the deadness of her. I just scream and scream.

Next I know I'm in the head-high, weed-grown field near where we're camped, and it feels like a few days have gone by, and an old woman holds the red thread that took the measure of my mother for the grave, and mourning is full under way, as is supposed to happen. In the distance is that derelict old ruin of a castle and the glint of water under moonlight staining the weatherless twilight.

Everyone merely stands and watches as our caravan burns. No one explains to me what's happening or why our home is being destroyed. Most people are weeping, some crossing themselves, the old ways merged with the new. But I can't feel a thing. I know I should but there's just this massive hole.

Ailín—Daidí—looks twenty years younger than in real life. He's handsome, the smell of him from distance like tobacco and fresh dug loam. His hands are as white as dead fish from where he's scrubbed them cleaner than I've ever seen, and his skin's free of the web-like *veins that stain his face now. A large canvas bag and a smaller old suitcase are beside him on the still-muddy ground where he kneels, keening, inconsolable, small memories of a life cut short, angling his face into lines of pain and grief.*

Someone has hold of my hand, but I don't look up, so I don't know who. I just look from my father to the fire, from my father to the fire.

Ailín crawls to me, so we're face to face and I can smell the whiskey on his breath. He's no longer weeping. Just concerned. Concerned and in deep concentration. 'You have to wake up now Róisín.'

'I am awake Daidí.'

'You're not, Róisín. Wake up. Róisín? Can you listen for once? Wake up now.'

Rose comes to consciousness with a start, her heart pounding, sitting up disoriented, rubbing her eyes and checking her phone. It is 3 AM and there are no messages.

'Jesus, Dad.' She pulls on her dark grey quilted jacket and beanie, tucks her cell phone in her pocket along with her keys, and drags the resisting front door closed behind her, shocked by the ice in a night of brutal cold.

In the alley Ailín rolls over, moaning in pain. He sits up with his knees bent and his arms wrapped around them, hurting and hardly daring to breathe. His eyes are wide with the knowledge he's a dead man, and he weeps silently for all the hopes that never eventuated. The sadness that never went away, blood bubbling at the corner of his mouth.

Rose searches all along the route he would have taken, until she reaches the Sailor's Rest's blackened windows and closed, barred door.

She doubles back, the torch from her phone shining down every dark lane and alley, until first she hears him and finally she finds him.

'Oh, Dad. Oh what have you done?' she whispers.

He tries to smile and fails, his voice a whisper of pain. 'I'm so sorry.'

'Stop talking.' She keys the triple emergency number into her phone.

'I need an ambulance.' She listens to instructions and doubles back to the street looking for the identification of the nearest address. 'The alley closest to 270 on Jackson, West R.' She shuts off her cell phone and returns to her father, cradling him, her face set in stone.

He coughs up blood and it dribbles down his chin. 'Take me home,' he manages.

'What? Dad no. You've got to go to the hospital'

'Bury me in the ground that holds your mother. Or near enough. Promise me.'

She's sure he's out of his mind with the things he's saying. The pain must be unbelievable from the savagery of the assault. She registers the wail of sirens even as she straightens to the body of her father, his violation and the effects of such a terrible bashing in stark juxtaposition to the strangely peaceful look in blank dead eyes.

She's sitting on the curb when the ambulance pulls up and two women, dressed in blue coveralls and carrying a *LifePak*, a little monitor-type machine, smile at her but go straight to the body, leaving the vehicle lights to illuminate the scene. The moment they hook him up to electrodes shoulder to hip, shoulder to hip, a police car cruises to a stop, its lights flashing a warning to the night.

One paramedic examines the screen while the other checks for a pulse, shining a light into Ailín's dead eyes, shaking her head and saying, 'pupils are fixed and dilated.'

People in pajamas, rough sleepers, lost folk living where they can and doing what they need do to survive in this part of the city, come in ones and twos, curious or scared, from the surrounding night, drawn by the sirens, hugging or crossing themselves and craning their necks to see, as people do. Something about witnessing.

While one police officer tapes off the crime scene, another calls the situation into the coms at his shoulder. He is approached by the younger paramedic and details are shared. The other paramedic detaches the *LifePak* from Ailín and stows the equipment back in the truck.

Rose comes to the cop with questions in her eyes but he says calmly and compassionately that no, the body can't be moved yet and that it's going to be a long night and is there anyone he can call. 'Sorry Ms. Wen, you have to come with me.'

She gives him Sam's number and allows herself to be drawn to the edge of the alley where she sits in the warmth of the heated police car.

Within twenty minutes two more vehicles park near the entrance to the alley, one a large HAZMAT that disgorges a forensics team.

Detective Inspector John Lannard could be any age but looks to be a strong, fit forty. Or fifty. Or some other age, not quite recognizable. He's tall and heavy-set—none of it fat—an unassuming black man with tired, compassionate eyes. He's in jeans, boots, a thick, high-neck sweater, a rabbit-skin lined all-weather parka and a dark grey beanie that covers his head, his ears and most of his forehead, causing his black eyes to seem blacker. He slides in beside Rose, pulls off a glove and presents her with his identification. He holds out a hand to her and Rose shakes it. Faded tattoos—some kind of indigenous or animal design—cover the whole of it, the ink marks disappearing into the cuff of his jacket, the texture of his skin like the leather of a worn drum. Firm, cool not cold, the pressure reassuring, as the gentle palm of it encloses her smaller one.

'Detective Inspector John Lannard, Ms. Wen.' His voice is ravine-deep, but gentle. Comforting. But she's in the cotton-wool of her trauma and shock and nothing much registers.

'He's my dad.' As though he would have no idea.

'There'll have to be an autopsy. The department will, of course, keep you in the loop about everything, but I'm sorry. I'm afraid this is going to take a very long time and we have to have a bit of an extended chat.' Her phone beeps with Sam's text. He's out on the main road, parking where he can.

'May I have your details so we can stay in touch? I'll need to talk to you tomorrow. I can come to wherever you are, you needn't think right now.'

Sam, in a *onesie* under a thick old dressing gown and sheepskin boots, is led to Rose who slides out of the car into the cold and into his arms.

'Sam Black Squirrel,' he tells Lannard, again his hand outheld, a curious sense of recognition hitting his gut as he looks the dark man in the eye. Dismissing it as déjà vu or something he could not have named.

'Sam's my friend from school. He's going to take me home. Am I allowed to go home?'

Sam holds her, looking over to where her father lies stiffening on the pile of garbage bags, as yet uninformed. Incredulous. Unable to know how to feel or what to do.

'Mister Black Squirrel—' Lannard begins while Sam has the practiced, patient look already plastered on his face, so used to being mocked. 'Is it possible for Rose to stay with you?'

'Janet's awake,' Sam says of his sister who shares the house with him. 'She's expecting us. Rose can stay as long as she likes, Detective. Is it okay if we go?'

'We can arrange a car to take Ms. Wen to pick up a few things from the residence in the morning, thanks Sam, so yes. We're going to need access to Ms. Wen's house for a few days however. To look around.'

Lannard's phone rings and he silences it with a swipe, his full attention focused, for now, on Rose's well-being, as the medical examiner arrives, photographers get to work, and multiple police attend the perimeter, where the crowd still waits in gloomy silence.

'Ms. Wen?'

'Yes?'

'I'll text you when the car is on the way in the morning, but it'll be around ten.'

She's non-committal. Even though it seems as if she has something to say by the look in her eyes, nothing comes out of her mouth. John has seen this before many times. A kind of denial. If a person says even one spare thing they're going to break.

'Try to get some sleep,' he suggests. 'We'll take care of your father.'

...

4

TÍR NA N'ÓG

THE GRAVEYARD IS IN THE SHADOW OF a small, lichen-covered stone chapel, half hidden by the mist of what might be rain, or could as easily be heavy fog in a landscape unknown to Rose. Funny how a body doesn't register the truth of the weather in a place that is alien to understanding. Celtic crosses mostly crowd the small patch of hallowed ground, some leaning as though to beg, take us back to the earth from which we were hewn. It's not even close to where her mother's ashes lie, soil and loam and peat and moss, hidden and unmarked in deep forest, some twenty miles to the south, but this is all Rose knows she can manage.

Today is misty, but the light is soft like never happens in the city, and the cream of still-young daffodils cluster in glimpses from within the long grass. An over-arching yew and a massive gnarly walnut tree, dark and broody, are strangely ominous-leaved, amongst the pale spring green of new growth, in the black of ravens and rooks, alive with the rustle of youngsters impatient to be flying.

Rose clutches a bunch of hand-picked wildflowers. She's in cargo pants, with a white shirt hanging loose, her quilted jacket collar pulled up against the damp, her copper hair tamed into a tight braid. Her face ghostly and drawn with the lines of fatigue. Her lips pinched and downturned.

Two distracted grave diggers lean on their shovels and mattocks, smoking fags, relaxed. Patient men with a steady, secure job. Off to one side of the gaping hole and the pile of fresh-turned earth, the plain wood coffin deep in the shadow of their work.

The priest is lean, almost gaunt, and seemingly quite young. His pale autumn-colored hair is cut close to his head and he's nothing much to look at, with a soft, unremarkable face and downcast eyes, making it impossible to read his expression. He wears a black cassock, and the purple funeral stola hangs like a measuring tape around the neck of a tailor. He shuffles the pages of what appears to be a prayer book, and he stands at the mouth of the grave, speaking with a contralto, almost feminine voice.

'And God said, *this is eternity, and all I've promised you; today your life on earth is past, but here it all starts anew*. And so it is. Today we commit the mortal remains of Aaron—'

'Ailín,' Rose corrects.

'Ailín, of course. Ailín Wen, into the loving arms of God the Father and eternity in paradise.

'And so Rose,' he smiles, shuffling haphazard at his notes, 'I've put together a little quote from the Steve Earle album, *Jerusalem*, as I thought it might be nice, our man liking the poetry and all.

'*A long time ago before the ice and the snow, there were giants that walked this land, and with each step they took, the mighty mountains shook, And the trees took a knee and the seas rolled in.*

Then one day they say the sky gave way, and death rained down, it made a terrible sound. There was fire everywhere and nothing was spared, that walked on the land or flew through the air, and when it all was over, the slate wiped clean with a touch, there god stood and he saw it was good, and he said, ashes to ashes and dust to dust.'

An uncomfortable silence evaporates his smile and Rose's frown like railroad tracks, separates her eyebrows, confused but not curious enough to ask why that.

'And so it is,' the priest concludes, 'that we commend Ailín into the hands of the mighty and long may he rest. Ashes to ashes, dust to dust, from this we come and to this we all return. May his soul rest in everlasting peace. Amen.'

'Amen,' say the men leaning on their shovels.

'Anything you'd like to add, Rose?' asks the priest.

She says nothing, but drops her little bouquet onto the coffin and walks away, head high, careless of her booted feet on wildflowers and glad for the fog.

Robin leans against the barky roughness of the walnut tree, observing. Wavering in and out of focus.

Rose walks up the slope leading away from the graveyard, towards the end of the one street town that defies the wild western ocean. A low rock wall keeps out the highest of tides and curraghs and black-sailed Hookers rock in the dark waters. A patience of gulls floats among the moored fishing boats. Near the corner of the street is a pub that's been here as long as the village. Locals, booze in their hands, smoke ciggies where it's legal, a few standing in clusters, some sitting at the little mismatched metal tables out in the rare dryness of the day. All notice the pale, pretty freckled redhead approaching, looking like she belongs here, but none know her.

Irish-themed knickknacks and postcards, pottery and hand-crocheted doilies, are displayed in the windows of the little shops for when the tourists come. The couple of small grocery stores are almost empty of people. The women in both the town's art galleries smile as she walks past. Walton's bodhràns rest on wooden handmade stands in the window of the creator, last cottage at the end of the sea-wall.

Rose wanders by the cluster of pub-goers and the stragglers fishing off the jetty, to a white-washed stone house on the street front with potted geraniums on window ledges, their vivid red flowers defiant of the cold, and where a salt-faded shingle creaking out from above the door reads *Mary Flynn's Bed and Breakfast*. Her mood is peculiar when she noticed the roof of the house, and the overhead power lines. Both are adorned with crows, silent except for the occasional youngster not yet understanding corvid etiquette at times like this.

She enters the freshly painted open front door, disheartened and cold, her hand raised in greeting to Mary Flynn, who sits in the day room watching *The Ellen Show* with the volume down, who turns and waves back. Mary takes in the look of the child of the dead stranger as Rose climbs the stairs. She sighs with an understanding known well in this part of the world because she, older than old but with only the merest hint of grey in her hair like threads, matching the color of her cardigan, was a girl during the Troubles. She understands that people never get over grief, empathizing with the hopelessness and emptiness that require no words. She fingers the necklace, that hangs from her throat like a rosary, of small bronze rings and bright black beads of faceted jet, singing softly under her breath. Something Gaelic. Fittingly soothing to the bewilderment blanketing the village.

As night falls, Robin sits on Ailín's grave sipping some peat-and-heather scented brew from a silver flask. After every mouthful he pours a little onto the fresh dirt.

'In nomini patri, et fili et spiritu sancti, old son.' He sits cross-legged on the damp soil for a moment before grinning and wiping at his mouth as though he'd eaten something long-dead. *Dear Mother Mercy I'm a sorry excuse for a mourner.* Wait. I'll do it again. He stands, legs apart, hands in his pockets

'Ah, see? *Once upon a midnight dreary, while I pondered weak and weary, over many a quaint and curious volume of forgotten lore, desolate yet all undaunted, on this desert land enchanted, on the morrow will he leave me, as my hopes have flown before, quoth the raven, nevermore...*'

He pushes his hat almost to the tips of his ears. 'We're done now, son. Lie gentle. I'll see she's not alone and lost without you.'

The pub looks small from the outside. It is crowded with villagers who talk in the Irish language that Rose doesn't understand, or else with accents so thick it might as well be. Laughing and flirting. Someone playing a low whistle even as the Cranberries *Dream Collection* plays through the speakers loud enough to make thinking tricky.

Curious eyes wash over her on the way to someone else. *Because,* she supposes incorrectly, *I'm drinking coffee in a bar.*

She sits at a little unsociable table closest to the corner that overlooks the reverse of the gilded lettering of *O'Riordan's*, and out into the fine misty rain, the poetry of the village with kids playing on the road like ghosts, heedless of the damp. She scrolls through the news on her phone, a plate pushed to one side and her cup, almost empty.

Robin opens and closes the door to an overhead tinkle, hardly noticed. He elbows his way to the bar mumbling, *sorry* and *hello* and *thanks*, and *sláinte mhaith*. He buys two pints of stout and carries them to Rose's table. He seats himself on the empty bench. 'The Guinness is like nothing you'll get anywhere else, have you been told?'

She figures it's just the local idiosyncrasy, so she doesn't want to be her usual acerbic self. Not yet, anyway. 'I'm waiting for somebody,' and she peers out the window.

He nudges the pint closer and tucks his flyway dark curls behind his ears, crossing his booted feet out in front of him. 'And you shall wait no longer.'

Rose is now exasperated at his audacity but she falters, confused. Familiarity like a dream repeating itself.

'Have we met?

'Couldn't say, sure.'

His index finger slides the pint glass a little closer still. Rose ignores it, so Robin clinks the two glasses together and takes a sip from both.

'To keep the faeries from swapping it for water when you're not looking,' he smiles. 'My name's Robin. How was the funeral?'

'What?'

'You have the look of the recently begraved.'

'It's bereaved. And how is this any of your business? Go away. Please.' She peers back out the window, becoming more embarrassed and angry when he doesn't move.

'*To feel is better than to know, and wisdom is a childless heritage. One pulse of passion - youth's first fiery glow - are worth the hoarded proverbs of the sage...* do you think that's fair to say?'

Just like that, and he's switched a light on inside her. 'That's Wilde.'

'I'm generally quite tame, truth be told,' he replies, intentionally guileless.

'No, Oscar Wilde. Never mind.' She fiddles with the zipper of her jacket, trying to get the two metal bits to join up as though her life depends on her doing so.

'Never?'

Rose drops her phone into her bag and readies to leave.

'It was a pleasure to meet you, Rose,' he adds.

She's slightly frightened and a bit confounded. 'And you know my name, how?'

'It's a small village. Not that often a beautiful stranger turns up with a dead man what doesn't live here and didn't drown or have his liver explode or get chewed up by the blades of his combine harvester. Any of those apply?'

She decides he's the village wise-guy and that she probably needs to get as far away from him, and this country for that matter, as she can so she ignores his last comments and makes her way through the crowd to the exit.

Robin leans back in his chair, reciting softly, '...*vex not thy soul with dead philosophy - have we not lips to kiss with, hearts to love and eyes to see?*' He sighs, realizing what he must do, and how it must all play out.

...

5

THAT STRANGE AND LOVELY MADMAN

HER ROOM UPSTAIRS IN THE bed and breakfast is beige and cheap, but pleasant enough having no memories she can sense. Its only embellishment is a wall-mounted television that she'll never turn on and, there must be a god after all, its own bathroom.

She removes the offense of a crucifix from above her pillows and slides it to the rear of the bottom drawer of her bedside table.

She lies on her back in the dark staring at the patterns on the ceiling above her, silhouettes cast by tree branches up close to the outer wall, the song of their scratching equally unnerving and enchanting in the soft night wind.

After what feels like hours, or maybe days, she gives in, sits up, switches on the bedside lamp and glances at the clock that glows 04:15. That time before dawn when most people die.

She gives up on sleep and gets out of bed. She pads to the sideboard and switches on the electric kettle, dropping a tea bag in a cup.

She drags herself to the bathroom, flicks on the light and scrutinizes her reflection in the mirror. Her hair a mess, her eyes tired and empty of shine. Just above a whisper, she says, 'So, now we are unburdened. No more worry or ceaseless chatter. No more endless fear that the house will burn him, or disease infirm him. How come we still don't feel anything?' She waits, sensing, not ever recognizing that the depression simmering just below the surface of apathy is one of dispossession and childhood trauma. 'Nothing. Snow and ice and the past buried along with him.'

She turns on the tap and splashes her face with cold water. 'Anyway, we're glad he's dead,' she whispers, drowning in her own untidy image, 'aren't we?' She runs her hands through her mane to untangle it, and rests the flat of her hands on the sink, before coming closer to her reflection and scowling.

'So here's what has to happen now, Róisín Wen. We go back to college and finish our degree. Do we sell the house? Live there? No.' She says all this aloud, a life-long, mumbling habit that has her convinced she's the only person who talks sense in her life. 'We get an apartment and think about the house later. We forget about love, and we teach.' She is exasperated by her messy, exhausted image.

'You listening to me?'

She flicks the light off at the switch. Takes her cup of tea to the bed. 'Some day something inspires us to write worthwhile poetry and we try to remember how to sleep.'

She leans back against the pillows, takes a few sips and puts the cup on the bedside table. 'And we forget about that strange and lovely madman, whatever his name was.'

She turns out the light, and lies flat on her back, sleep claiming her despite herself. Dreaming another vivid dream. The first she'll ever remember that isn't the repeat of the death of her mother.

I'm with Robin in a forest with deep green undergrowth of ivy and bracken, with twisty-limbed trees stark against the haze, all bathed in an autumn twilight the colors of old amber and the pewter of early mist. Trees and ferns, lichen-covered boulders, gorse and wild roses hide all but the slightest view of both a lake, its surface like molten bronze in the light of the westering sun and the distant tall, derelict stone ruin of something long-forgotten.

Critters to whom this is home are gathered. Badger and deer, fox and stoat, blue-black glossy corvids in the raggedy bare lichen-stained branches, keeping safe distance from a bunch of snowy owls. Wild ponies and great-horned black-faced sheep behaving for a change, realizing the presence of legend in their midst. The shadow of the ruin of that stone tower darkening against the twilight, still day.

I have my back against a tree half hidden amongst the bracken, ivy, henbane and wild foxgloves, oblivious to the wonder of these surroundings and reading from a book of blank pages. He's here but I ignore him. He's too close for me to be comfortable.

He squats, his eyes bright and strange. 'Is't truth that speaks a man who says he only speaks in lies?' he asks, quoting someone I can't quite remember.

I meet his gaze with all the defiance I can. 'Always riddles with you Puck. Nasty mind games, little dares.'

'Ah, then. You know me well, but have we met before?' He drops to the ground beside me and stretches out on his side.

'I've not met you, Puck,' and my voice tastes of venom or something dead, 'but men like you and many will again.'

I snap the book shut. Brother wolf, his head on his front paws, mindless of the coterie of mice close at hand, is now more curious than hungry. 'You find me when I'm far away, somewhere within my mind. And you pester me with every trap and trick that you can find.'

Still playful, he changes tactic. 'I'm curious, though you're clearly in a mood, sweet loveless girl, you know my name. To not grant yours seems rude.'

'I don't know your name, you fool. I simply know you're known as Puck.'

He touches my face hesitantly and I feel the need to run like he's that wolf in sheep's clothing in the story books. But I don't. His eyes are unreadable. He says, 'I see you fault these things for which I'm blamed. I'm disturbing and offending you, for which I am ashamed. I simply wanted you to see me. Not the trickster but the man.'

He drops his hands into his lap. Sad. Not even returning the call of the hawk above him or responding to the tsunami of bats that darken the perennial presence of an opalescent sky. 'But you dislike the very spirit that makes me who I am. You stole my heart the moment that you fixed me with your stare: eyes of pure molten emerald: devastating. Deep and rare.'

He stands and shakes his left leg, all pins and needles because I know, intuitively, he's not used to being this still for so long, never seemingly a one for patience.

He pulls at the damp, brown, last-summer's leaves and twigs stuck throughout his hair. 'You referred to all these other men and how closely you think I compare, and you figure the gifts I offer are only riddles, games and dares.'

He has every intention of walking away but thinks of something else and turns back to me, incredulous.

'Do you not want a man for whom your mind might matter too? A man who you can play with or a man to challenge you? All I sought was to sit with you and to maybe share a moment. But the only piece of you you'd share was your contempt and judgment. That's very bitter.'

It's as though I'm only just seeing him for the first time. And even though I refuse to give him the satisfaction of seeing me cry I am, as usual, ashamed. Robin falters, horrified, his hand clutching at his heart.

'I suppose it makes no difference, now,' I add, 'what I say or what I do. But I've never met an othering, *before my encounter here with you.'*

I don't know what he's thinking. Do I care? I get up off the barky, leaf-littered ground clutching my empty book as though my very life depends on it.

'We're told stories and told how to act and I know now that's not fair, but I guess I never thought that what was myth might think to care. And I'm sorry. I truly am.' I walk right up his face. 'I do think challenging and playful are important in a man. If you can excuse me I will rectify my prose and I will gladly introduce myself. I'm known as Rose.'

She wakes to buttery sunshine piercing the slats of the fake-wood *Ikea* blinds. She's tangled in the bed covers, the dream as real as the morning. She feels the exhaustion of one who's run a marathon, chased by nightmares. Naked, she half-staggers to the shower.

She manages to keep down the breakfast that Mary makes, of toast and Kerry Gold butter with home-made marmalade and a big mug of instant coffee. She packs her phone, her notebook and a warm jumper despite the sunshine, this being Ireland. She closes the gate behind her and navigates the cobbled road. She wanders the village, her new camera in its soft neoprene case hanging from her shoulder, thinking to record her time here. For who? For her children? *Stop it*, she thinks, sure she will never have any.

First thing she does is explore one, then the other of the tiny galleries, entranced by an entire collection of teapot art, depictions of the grief and wildness of distraught widows of drowned fishermen. Telling in a visual way how the sea takes, regardless of religion or love.

In a park, down by the little canal that cuts the village in two, with a Saint Bridget's Well at its heart she throws in a handful of coin. Not wishing.

Without even thinking or intending she ends up back at the graveyard wandering at random, reading the epitaphs and wondering at all the dead children. She startles a fox, its pelt thick with new spring fur the color of copper. It sits fearlessly, watching her, seeming to smile before bleeding back into the shadows like it was never there.

Unintentionally, she wanders inexorably towards the fresh black earth of her father's new grave with no headstone and no intention of one, mounded beneath the gnarled and threatening yew tree. A story-telling of enormous well-fed crows crowd along the overhanging branches, silent but observant.

One alights on a Celtic cross beside her and *ack-acks* loudly, its beady white eye watching her from its tilted head, as if reminding her of every accusation she's leveled at her father. Rose, unnerved because she understands, and refuses to either want to or be intimidated, leaves the dead to the dead.

Within the hour, around two o'clock in the afternoon, she has distanced herself from both the black birds and her memories, to be freer in a way than she remembers. Ever. Or so she deludes herself into thinking. Something to do with this air, perhaps.

She meanders a narrow dirt-packed track stippled with the hoof prints of one herd or other, on their way to a byre. She's high above the windswept bay but deep enough amongst the folds of the grassy, drystone walled countryside to feel safe from the possibility of falling, idly and irrationally taking photos of scenery.

She has the viewfinder to her eye adjusting the depth of field at the vision of a mine shaft in the distance, a huddle of ponies in the foreground all staring at her as though she is a predator. She isn't even aware of the old *Massey Ferguson* tractor that passes her before the rumble of a motorbike as it pulls up. She startles. So much so that she stumbles off balance, falling into the gorse and briar at the side of the road, disguising the dry stone wall and luckily cushioning a fall that could have hurt her had she struck it. She winces however, where the thorns pierce her. She works at gaining her footing when a leather-gloved hand extends towards her.

It's Robin. He wears a pack on his back and he idles the motorcycle, leaning it on its kickstand. 'Nice day for being in the bushes, Róisín.'

She lets go the hand as though it has burnt her. 'Stalking is illegal, you know.'

She manages to extricate herself from the brambled foliage, gets her footing and walks away a little.

'Wait up, I'm joking. Okay then. No.'

'No what?' Her fists are on her hips.

'Nothing much sometimes.' He pulls his gloves off and stuffs them in the back pocket of his jeans. 'Other times I'm masterful with knowing stuff.'

'Whatever with the word games. Can you just go away?'

'Sorry. Can we start again? Please? Do you want to get a really good coffee?'

He's bright and cheery. And handsome.

'Where? There's nowhere.'

'Next village.' He straddles the motorcycle. 'Five minutes down the road. Much nicer crowd. Great cafe. See? I can be normal. Get on.' He unhooks a spare helmet. 'It'll be fun, I promise.'

'I don't know you.' Old habits, but the air shimmers as Robin casts a small spell. Rose relaxes.

'I can take my clothes off and you can search me for weapons and the like.'

He drops his backpack and starts pulling off his sweater, exposing a muscled torso and the hint of a dark and intricate tattoo.

'Stop that. I'll come all right? Just no, to the clothes off.'

Robin adjusts himself, stuffs the pack into one of the panniers and again holds out the helmet. Rose pulls it on and tightens the chin strap, mounting the pillion seat.

'I'll go slow for you,' he yells over his shoulder, snorting back a laugh.

Rose's arms circle grudgingly around his waist, oblivious to the jibe.

He toes the motorcycle into gear, ignoring her venomous mind.

...

6

A SILVER PENTAGRAM, A DIAMOND-STUDDED TOOTH

INSIDE, THE CAFÉ IS ACTUALLY A bookshop, but for pre-read books, nothing new, and the cafe is just a bonus. There's a middle, an upstairs and a downstairs, all of it peopled with adults of every age and ethnicity. Bookish. Exotic and nerdish. Beat poets and bohos. Bearded, hijab'd and goth, gender neutral and carelessly sensual.

Busy, engrossed, talking low in pairs or small clusters or seated alone behind books and laptops. Artists with pencils, pastels or charcoal. Occasional tourists out of their depth in such an unexpectedly diverse *unIrish* establishment. An old Dire Straits song sending shivers along Rose's spine like a chill wind, from the enchantment of Mark Knopfler's guitar riff from the track *Brothers in Arms*, reminding her of mist covered mountains and to never forget what's important in life.

A starling of soft chatter buzzes lightly but many also study, read, write notes and search shelves. Coffee tables, chairs, settees, nooks form a labyrinth of comfort.

'What'll you have?' asks Robin. 'My treat.'

'You can treat me the first one, Robin Whatever-your-name-is. An espresso, strong. Thanks. But if there's ever another I won't be owing you.' She's smiling at her sense of self-establishment but feeling out of place in her dark grey, quilted jacket, red wool beanie and cargo pants. A sensation she is not used to. Surprised.

'Grab us somewhere to sit. I'll find you.'

She almost disappears in the downy, overstuffed, once plush dark blue velvet theatre settee, but realizes the ridiculousness of the effect and stays put, happily bathing in the ambience until Robin plops down beside her with the coffees.

'I had no idea.' She's enchanted despite herself, brighter than she can ever remember having been, like a thirsty adventurer who strayed too far into a desert finding an unexpected oasis.

'They're mostly writers, students and the like,' he explains, stirring sugar into his cup. 'They come down from the city for the artists-in-residence retreat just up the road and across the bay, at Inishlacken. Do you live here and I've been blind, or are you just visiting, Rose?'

'I fly home in two days.' She tastes the coffee. Surprised at how good it is.

'So where's home?'

'A thousand miles away across the sea. An old fur trading city named New Rathmore.'

'Hence the funny accent.' He's grinning, but Rose ignores what she figures is a taunt. He shifts in his seat, very aware of just how far he can push her, but she recovers her cool.

'So, Robin? Like in Redbreast? Goodfellow? Hood?'

'You remembered. No. Like in Kipling.'

'Robin Kipling.'

'Now you're getting personal, my *Lady of Shalott*.'

'What?

'You.'

'Why?'

He watches her, eyes teasing from beneath dark, too-long-for-a-man eyelashes, cocking his head to one side and reminding her of the crows around her father's grave.

'She's under a curse because if she looks directly at Camelot an unknown doom will befall her. So she watches the world through a mirror and weaves what she sees into a magic web. The shadowy glimpses of life beyond the tower tempt her to look, although she knows that to do so will bring the curse into being. One day, seeing Lancelot in her mirror, she realizes how sick of her destiny she truly is. Of knowing the world only through shadows and reflections.'

'Is that how you see me?' It irritates her that he should assume her to be like this.

He leans close. Intimate. '*And in the lighted palace near, died the sound of royal cheer; and they crossed themselves for fear, all the Knights at Camelot; but Lancelot mused a little space, he said, she has a lovely face; God in his mercy lend her grace, the Lady of Shalott.*'

Rose is momentarily enchanted before laughing it off. She sips her coffee and bores into him with wire in her gaze. Robin pulls back but does not drop his eyes.

Then she visibly softens. 'I love Tennyson. Robin. I'm sorry. I swear I'm not usually so temperamental. I just—'

Robin is buoyant, inching closer. *'Do not swear! Although I joy in thee.* Róisín, never apologize. Can we make a pact? Otherwise I won't believe you even when you mean it.'

'This is getting way, way too intense for me. Can we talk about something mundane and trivial? She looks around the cafe seeking the bathroom. 'I'll be back in a minute.'

He stands and directs both arms towards a far wall, like an airplane attendant preparing to give emergency exit instructions. No one else notices. As though he's not there or else they're so used to peculiar people he does not register to them.

She wends her way into the cramped toilet, its walls plastered with old newspaper from years gone, paint half-scraped from the back of doors, but clean and somewhat chic in a way Rose does not comprehend, having only ever known shabby.

When she returns Robin's squeezed up in the corner of the couch, enveloped, like a possum in a pouch. She wonders if perhaps she should be asking him to take her home as this is all very intimate and way too friendly for her to really relax. She sits, determined to try.

'Right, so. I have questions, Rosie—'

'Not my name. Not ever. Rose or Róisín.' She reacts in a subdued but haughty voice, reminded of Emmet in the hypocorism and hating the memory.

'Rose. Sorry. Róisín. So. Rose. Can I ask you something?'

'What, Robbie?'

He is delighted that she bested him, but then, unexpectedly, she experiences an inexplicable stabbing pain in her gut at the way he says her name, as though touching on the memory of someone deep in the shadows of an abandoned mansion in her imagination. Robin notices but ignores it. On track with his own agenda.

'Will you inform me of what you wish for, while you live and breathe?' He drops his booted feet to the floor in case someone suggests that he's pushing the rules way too far.

She thinks. Not about what to say but wondering. Disturbed at how relaxed she is. So much so that she's so willing to tell him. 'Ah, two things. Once there would have been three but I'm all grown up and sensible now.'

'I'll remember that.'

'I'm in my last year at college.'

Robin becomes serious. Intent and excited. Leaning closer, dipping his head to listen, his interest seeming sincere, his attention genuine. 'Studying what?'

'Literature. I want to teach it. Teach others to write great things.'

'Not write great things yourself?'

'Didn't you hear me?'

'Why not?'

'I want to teach. To inspire others.'

'Is it that you don't have any stories?'

He comes across as incredulous and Rose doesn't quite know how to respond. She knots her hands to prevent herself from picking up her bag and walking out, already not knowing who she'll be without him.

Changing imperceptibly as change often does.

'I have stories.'

'Real ones or made up ones?'

'Both.'

'Please tell me a real one. A 'Rose' story. A once-upon-a-time-when story.'

'That's my name. There's a true story for you.'

'What?'

She sips her coffee, smiling at the girl with the dyed black hair, red lips and the silver pentagram around her neck, who smiles back, a front tooth studded with a diamond.

'Wen,' she says, returning to the game.

'When what? What're you telling me Rose? Am I daft?'

'Wen.'

'What?'

'My name. Rose Wen. W.E.N.'

'You serious?'

'Robin Kipling, I'm Rose Wen.'

'I'm really confused now.'

'Why?'

'Because W.E.N. is a gypsy name.'

Rose downs the dregs in her cup and pulls her beanie deeper over her hair, pushing the russet wisps inside. 'Will you please take me home?'

'What did I say? Oh Rose, please don't be angry. *If I offended thee it was not my wont but a sprite in passing nipping at my tongue.* Please. What's the second thing?'

She sits again, but on the edge of the seat. 'What?'

'You said there were two things and a third that was not to be spoken. Kind of like a spell.'

'I do write. Poetry,' she admits, edgy like a deer before a predator, 'and a few short stories. But they're not good. And they're private. And staying that way.'

He moves close enough to kiss her. 'You want another coffee?

Rose pulls back, intimidated. 'I prefer you better when you're an idiot and I don't like you,' she lies. 'Are you hitting on me?'

'I'm trying to.'

Rose considers this. Respecting his honesty but much too insecure to flirt. 'Well, don't.'

He is distraught at the rejection.

'Can I show you my secret place?' He pulls on his jacket and takes the gloves from his back pocket.

'This isn't it?'

'This was to impress you the first time.'

'And the secret place?'

'It's a piece of the magic. The important one of the two. Coat, Wen.'

Rose pokes her arms into the sleeves of her jacket. 'Okay. I trust you.'

Robin's moods are like nothing she's known except for her father when he was younger. Quick darting and unpredictable. There are tears in his eyes.

'You alright?' she asks, confused.

'That's the most important thing anybody could ever say.'

'What? Trust?'

Robin takes Rose's hand as though at a courtly dance. He bows and his lips brush it lightly.

Sunset, soft and dusky with sea spray and twilight mist. Robin parks the motorcycle beside a barely discernible track and pulls his pack from the panniers, tugging to get it free, it bulging more than when they arrived at the cafe. They travel on foot through the iridescent greens exuding from the forest, of rowan, beech and oak, and arrive at a lake just as mist insinuates itself, wraithlike, over the timeless, glassy surface. Rose is awed.

Robin runs to the edge of the lake and breathes great lungs full of the air of decomposing foliage.

He returns to her, his face one of delight. He sits cross-legged on the spruce-needle-strewn area of the ground at the base of the huge conifer. He opens his pack and pulls out a bottle of wine and a large paper bag containing cling-wrapped sandwiches. He puts everything on the ground and rummages in the bag till he finds a Swiss army knife with which to uncork the bottle.

'Did you plan this?'

'While I waited for the coffee I raced into the shop next door. Just in case.'

'What about the sandwiches?'

'They were for me but you interrupted the day. We supping together, my Lady of Shallot?'

Rose settles beside him and pulls her camera from its case.

'No!' He puts his hand over the lens. Rose startles. He's being strange again.

'What's wrong?'

'Please. Not here.'

'It's only for me.'

Robin is unshakable. 'Nothing's ever just for only one person, Rose. Will you not take any photographs? I'll beg.'

She stows the camera away, determined not to be offended. 'So where are the glasses?'

'Oops.'

'Nice to know you're a human. Give it here then.' He hands her the cab sav and she swigs. There's an uncomfortable silence and Robin fidgets. 'You going to share that?'

Rose passes him the wine. 'What is this place?'

'Home,' he smiles.

'Where's your house then smarty pants?'

Robin closes his eyes and frowns, summoning up the words from his archives. '...and I would stand, if the night blackened with a coming storm, beneath some rock, listening to notes that are the ghostly language of the ancient earth, who make their dim abode in distant winds... thence did I drink the visionary power; and deem not profitless those fleeting moods of shadowy exultation.'

'Wordsworth. You don't really live here do you?'

Robin's shocked. 'I never lie, Róisín Wen.'

'Where's your house? Do you have a family? Where did you learn all the poetry? Where did you go to school?'

'What? Right. Ah, close by and I do. A big one. And from them. And I got taught at home. Now enough about me.'

'Not nearly enough.'

'I promise to tell you everything before you fly away. I'm nasty that way, but I don't lie ever, Rose. Not ever.'

'Neither did my father, despite everything. I'm sorry.'

'It's still not time for sorry, but I really, really, *really* want to know about you and your life.'

'Why?'

'Lots of reasons. You're beautiful, you're clever, you know poetry. You're from somewhere else and will abandon me. And I'll have nothing or I'll have a story.'

'Can't I give you a photo instead?'

'They trap a person so that they never seem to change. Traps end in regret and I don't agree with regret. Stories are different, especially when they're not written down.'

She's confused.' But you learned all that poetry.'

'I was *told* all that poetry.'

Rose takes a minute to digest what he said. 'You serious? Of course, you don't lie.'

Robin is cheerful as he unwraps the sandwiches. He holds one out to her. She takes it, her mind working. 'Can you read and write?'

'You're funny. It's a thing my family does. Remember stuff.'

'You all do it then?'

'We do.'

'I think I'd like your family.'

He takes a big bite of his sandwich and chews, stalling.

'Ah. You can. You can meet them if you want, just not right away.' He swallows a swig of wine and hands the bottle back to her. 'There's a condition.'

'I should have known.'

'Your story is the price.'

'Does it have to be factual?'

'Do you tell lies, Wen?'

He bothers her but she refuses to bite. 'An edited version, then?'

'That'll do, although I don't mind. I could listen to you forever; you must know that by now.'

She ignores how unnerved he causes her to feel. 'Well, we were Travelers but a long time ago…'

Owlets, four pre-flight youngsters, peer down from the hole in the trunk of the tree above their heads, while a hare the size of a small horse tears at the grass nearby, careless of both fox and ferret. Faster than either if it comes to a chase. 'But my father took to the drink. He got so he couldn't look after himself. Only work in his stupid garden, watch television or go to the pub. And ramble.'

'But he put you through school, did he not?'

'I put me through school. When I was thirteen I got a job after hours. Then later I won a scholarship.'

'I'm impressed.'

'Don't be. All I have are my books and unspoken opinions.'

'You could have given up.'

Rose is bitter. She hears herself. She can't stop from being forthright. She'll best him by not lying either. 'No. That was never an option. I could never have been like him.'

'Did you not love him a little?'

'He was pathetic.'

'So sad.'

'It's just life.'

In the dusk of mid evening, the motorcycle pulls up in front of Rose's lodgings and Robin switches off the engine. Rose unstraps the helmet and pushes her mad red curls away from her face, now sun-blushed amongst the freckles, aglow despite herself. Him running his fingers through his dark, flying-in-all-directions-hair. 'Will I see you tomorrow?'

'Can we go for coffee at the same place? I'd like to look at the books this time.'

'Ten?'

'Ten. I'll meet you out front here.'

'Have you got a pen?' He waits, averting his eyes at her scrutinizing of his possible motive. He studies his boots instead, in case of rejection.

Rose takes one from her jacket pocket and Robin holds out his hand. 'For your phone number, Wen, if you've a mind to give it.'

Rose turns his hand over, almost too aware of both the calluses at the base of his fingers and the softness of the pad beneath his thumb, and she writes on his wrist, her own pulse thudding beneath his.

Like storm turning to sunshine he grins. He toes the bike into gear and slowly ups the throttle. He drags the soles of his boots along the unpredictable surface of the ground as he rides the cobbled street and rounds the curve in the road. Rose watches till he's out of sight, pensive and bewildered by her unprecedented reaction to this twist of fate.

At just after eleven that night Rose is awake writing in her notebook by the light of the bedside lamp. Her phone rings.

'Hello?'

'It's Robin.'

'It's very late.'

'I had a wonderful day.'

She pulls at the hair tie and shakes her hair loose.

'Me too.'

'Night, Wen.'

'Night, Kipling.'

She disconnects. She sleeps without dreaming, surprised by the morning light.

...

7

THE DEVIL, YOUR HONOR

IN THE POLICE HEADQUARTERS INTERVIEW room in New Rathmore Central, John Lannard, eyes tired and gritty, sits at the table opposite Billy Shando still in his worn, stained parka with his fingerless gloves and the dark grey felt hat pulled halfway down to his eyes. As far as anyone can ascertain, just another witness to the abuse from the strangers who may or may not have killed Ailín Wen.

Coffee, hardly touched, has gone cold. Forgotten in its chipped white mug.

A laptop is between the two, and a camera set to video at the end of the table. Two plain clothed police are occupied with its function. Everyone except Billy Shando are relaxed.

Lannard turns the laptop towards Billy and nods at one of the officers who activates the camera. Lannard directs his attention to its blinking red eye.

'I am identifying myself as John Lannard, Detective Inspector, New Rathmore Metropolitan Central Police Department. Warrant number 21DI312070. I am authorized by the County of Blackwell to conduct this interview on behalf of the Office of the Department of Justice of Blackwell County under the jurisdiction of the state. Today is October 29, at 15:21 hours. This interview is with Mr. William Shando of Unit four, fifteen Ellis Road Towers, New Rathmore, West. Thank you for coming, Mr. Shando.'

'Billy. My friends call me Billy. Or sometimes Bill. Or Father Bill. Or brother Bill. Do you always wear that?' He is indicating Lannard's beanie, a fixture with the cop as though the cold won't leave him long enough to remove it, or else a simple statement of individuality.

'Mr. Shando, you were at the Sailors Rest Hotel on July fifteenth. The night Mr. Wen was murdered. Is that true?'

'Billy. Or Bill. Sorry. I was.'

'And was there an altercation inside the hotel that night between Mr. Wen and another man?'

'Is 'Mr. Wen' Ailín?'

'Ailín Wen, yes.'

'Am I in trouble?'

The police in the room shift, in order to appear relaxed. The officer at the camera end of the table sits down, seemingly bored. A ruse.

'Can you describe the events of that evening? Was there an altercation?'

Billy tells a version of what happened that night, referring to the pack of aggressive strangers as *hard men.*

'Can you explain what you mean by that, Mr. Shando?'

'Sorry. I'm from Limerick. Thereabouts, anyway. I grew up with stories of the hard men. They're not human, so. Heavy boys. Like hunting hounds. Beat you for a pocket watch if you didn't give them the time a day. Cold iron in their hearts instead a blood. Fuck me, you're a big feller.'

Lannard redistributes his weight on the chair, decidedly uncomfortable with the way this is going. 'Were you intoxicated on the night of the alleged murder of Ailín Wen?'

'The drink was in me, I won't lie. Doesn't make me an eejit.'

'Take a look at the faces on the screen please. Just scroll the image to your left to get to the next one. If you recognize any of the men who verbally harassed Ailín Wen on the night of his death could you say aloud *I recognize this man.* For the camera.' That soft, low voice somehow more intimidating than if he'd been aggressive in that good cop, bad cop technique.

Billy scrolls. He does so for several minutes. He stops. 'I recognize this man.'

'Note for the record William Shando is implicating Thomas Brodie Reed. To Billy he says, 'He was indicted for car theft and D & D. But never for anything violent, Mr. Shando. He was known as a religious man. A strict Catholic. Are you certain?'

'He was with them and laughing when the other feller took the piss out of Ailín.'

'Keep scrolling please, Billy.'

Billy flicks past mug shot after mug shot for several minutes and then looks up at Lannard, moving only his eyes. Terror.

'Billy? Are you okay?'

A stain spreads at the crotch of Billy's trousers.

'You found the man?'

Billy flicks the screen faster and faster so that whoever's image affected him is long gone. Then he closes the laptop, pushing it from himself.

'He'll come after me now.'

'Who? Billy, who is he?

'I think it's best to assume he's the Devil, your honor.'

The uniformed police officer becomes aware of what is happening at the same time. He speaks into his coms, requesting medical assistance. They are there within two minutes.

Outside the bed and breakfast that afternoon, Mary Flynn is in the small front yard, trowel in her pocket, secateurs in her hands, dressed as though for an occasion, necklace of old jet beads and bronze rings jangling with each movement. She incises cleanly at the dead or dying branches of some geraniums, planting others. Digging in the large terracotta pots to loosen the soil. She wipes her hands, satisfied, just as the sound of the motorcycle rounds the corner, gaining her attention as it navigates the roughness of the cobbles and pulls up at the curbside out front.

'I'll put the kettle on, shall I?' she asks as Rose dismounts. 'Is it for one or both of you?'

'Robin's heading off but I'd love some of your tea.'

Mary straightens her back and purposely looks the other way as Robin hooks his arms around Rose's shoulders, their bodies almost touching.

Rose is sure the spread of heat must show on her face. Her shallow breathing, like him, loud. Robin breaks the tension with a toothy smile. 'There's a bit of a get-together tonight. Family and friends. You don't have to come if you don't want.'

Rose almost succeeds at being in control. 'Are you inviting me?'

'You don't have to come.'

'Do you want me to come?'

'I do. And things start off around sunset.'

'What should I wear?'

'I'm a man. What would I know? You're beautiful like you are.'

She kisses his cheek and walks towards the lodging. Robin's hand goes to the spot she touched, in astonishment.

'See you in a couple of hours,' she calls over her shoulder.

He's unable to move until the door closes behind her. Facing the footpath, he is aware only of the cobbles of the old road in front of him. He shakes his head, admonishing himself, *what are you doing you fecken faerie?*

Thunder rumbles from a cloud-gathering evening. 'Enough of that, now,' he whispers to the sky and the rising storm. He straddles the motorcycle and kicks over the engine. The wind dies.

. . .

They arrive at the track's end and enter the forest on foot. It is just past sunset and the sky is a pale indigo, a sliver of fingernail moon rising above the tree line to the east.

They jump fallen branches and clamber under heavy overhangs, he and Rose hand in hand. A clearing allows them to walk without care of brambles and broken glass. The roundhouse tower broods amongst briars, thistles and yellow-headed woad. Robin leads them both towards the vaulted entrance from which light streams and Rose pulls back, confused.

'A ruin, Robin?'

'They're eccentric is all. They hold their parties here at midsummer.'

'You didn't say anything about a party, Robin. Look at me.' She gestures wildly at herself.

'What? You're grand, Rose.'

'But—'

'It'll be fine. Trust me.'

'Robin!'

'Be brave, my Lady of Shallot.'

He removes a silver flask from an inside jacket pocket, unscrews it and takes a swig. He shudders as the liquid hits him. He passes it to Rose who tastes the liquor, a honey and peat-scented mead and she wonders, just briefly, if this isn't all a very dumb idea. Robin replaces the flask and takes her by the hand, leading her towards the impossibly lit height and breadth of an ancient roundhouse, built on a man-made hill, raised up from the heart of the earth sometime in the last five thousand years.

The inside is impossible and Rose is wide awake. Isn't she? This isn't a dream, is it?

She is assaulted by a flood of sound, light, music and the vision of so many exotic, unexpected people of every ethnicity and gender, eccentricity and individuality.

They gyrate to the music, drink, laugh and partake of sumptuously presented delights. Some are clad in the velvet, lace and breast-enhancing corsetry of Renaissance fashion. Others are formal in black tie and evening gown but with piercings or body modifications. Others are dreadlocked and tattooed. Gothic black. Skate punk. Dangerous.

The ceiling can't be seen although a dozen ornate crystal chandeliers, aglow with an incalculable number of candles are suspended from somewhere in the gloom high above.

On stage four DJs groove with electronic equipment. They synchronize with a five-piece rock band and musicians playing traditional Irish instruments along with big, sweaty men on a vast array of percussion.

At odd angles are other levels: some with tables and chairs, others with bars worked by scantily clad bartenders. Dancers move in ornate gilded faux-cages that dangle from high above, while aerial artists work a spectacle of circus-style agility on silks and hoops.

Mezzanines are accessed by staircases with banisters of ornately-carved and polished wood. Twisted wrought iron spirals lead into an unseen above. What walls there are, are mirrored. Beyond them, fathomless dark.

Rose understands now. Something beyond her concept of reality is unfolding and a deep, inner conversation encompasses what? Her entire life? Yes. Here it is then. Everything she has denied. She's in a story.

None of this is real. She may as well enjoy it.

The clue for her, to the mystery of everything she has studied and learned, of what the poets mean of wonder and love, and muses and mythology, is that all these revelers are masked. In ornate representations of animals and birds. Uncountable species, butterfly to creatures unrecognizably alien, as though conjuring and summoning these intelligences to participate in the dance, or perhaps to suggest we never were what we convinced ourselves we are. Or are supposed to be.

Stories her father told over the years, that she mocked or dismissed as fantasy, of seal men and deer women, of owls and ravens really being people, and people them like phantoms through her mind. Of gypsies like her, of their lore, of lost and drowned lands off the western coast from before the monks came and killed the heart of things. Their demand for shame and guilt. Their bitter tongues and threats of a hereafter that was nothing like her people knew to be true.

She remembers reading *Buffalo Gals Won't You Come Out Tonight*, about a little girl who died and whose spirit was aided and educated by other species, and who took her home when the sickness of being lost and confused was healed. She wonders, briefly, if she, too, is dead. Did something happen to her? Is this the underworld or the afterlife? The Ireland of her ancestors? Could a person truly know? Is this the fairyland of the stories?

She keeps her questions to herself, riding the experience, because there are no answers, just like the death of her mother and now her father. Why? Both killed so violently and pointlessly. It was pointless, wasn't it? Is this her hope of more than that? She has never known such fear, but she is also aware of the still quiet inner voice that says, *at least you're feeling something, Rose.*

She's lightheaded and dizzy, and Robin catches her before she falls.

She cannot focus clearly and a haze or sheen of something akin to rainbow clings to the air like when the sun hits a waterfall or shines through the mist. Like an ethereal and localized *na gealáin thuaidh*— aurora borealis.

Her casual, forgettable attire has morphed into a revealing, spider-web-like black, leaving nothing of her body to the imagination, with diamonds, like dew, dangling on the ends of silken threads as the gown pools, winter rain, around her ankles. *Of course*, she thinks, going with whatever this is now.

She turns a sensual and knowing look to Robin who strips off his jacket and T shirt, his eyes locking with hers. The ink she noticed briefly on the day she met him is a vast tree tattooed intricately over his torso, the branches passing up to his shoulders and trailing down his back.

'Sorry I am, Róisín,' he shuffles, mumbling, as though shy.

'This is not real the way I think of real, is it Robin?'

He takes her elegantly by the arm and leads her onto the dance floor. 'If I'd told you, even though it's true I never lie, you wouldn't have believed me and so we'd never be here. Doing this.'

'Was it that drink? Or has it been like this— How long has it been like this? And what, then, are you? Are you an angel or something? I'm dead, aren't I?'

'Don't be daft, Rose. There's no such thing as angels.' He snorts a laugh. Not sarcastically, just amused she should have come to that conclusion. 'Define death when it's way too long and boring a technicality. You're alive. Gorgeous, wild and wondrous free, Róisín.'

He rubs at the stubble on his chin, biting his cheek. 'What would you have done if you'd learned I'm other than a man?'

'I see a man,' she says, despite herself. 'But why this? Charades, is it?'

'It's as real as either of us, Róisín Wen of the Travelers. If you think hard enough you'll remember. Tonight is twixt the light and the dark of the seasons, you understand. Willie Shakespeare knew. Even despite the story of them two fellers of the queen that your father tells every so often at the pub, about a pig and an old woman.'

'So you're—They're—' She rolls her eyes in disbelief.

Robin laughs from the very pit of his belly, eyes shut, and head thrown back. He pulls her into an embrace she is not expecting and she thrusts him away. He bends his head, still smiling, and looks her in the eye. 'Can't say the *f* word out loud, now can I? Not now mortals have displaced it with something very cruel and silly. Dance with me. And Róisín, don't eat a thing, and don't drink a thing, in here, at all. Do promise me.'

Rose searches his face for duplicity and it's just not there. Then she scrutinizes the experience of the gala. Awareness dawning. Robin never lies. Is she dead? Is this an afterlife? Or was there some strange mushroom in that sweet liquor he fed her out in the forest?

'I promise,' she answers.

He takes her by the hand and leads her into the crowd, to a subtle ripple of whispers. Because she shouldn't be here. Because Robin has broken the rules again.

The murmuring crescendo of the orchestra and DJs ceases. The fiddler and the cellist play alone. An ancient, haunting, otherworldly, tune.

He kisses her. And she returns the kiss.

Like the crashing of thunder from the electrical storm drenching the forest and the village nearby, overwhelming the music, is the high pitched, urgent wail of a siren. The revelers turn, like swallows in formation, towards a darkness.

Everything and everyone, with the exception of Rose and Robin, spins, nauseatingly.

'Dear Mother Mercy,' Robin mumbles, frantically. Knowing it's pointless, wanting to deny what is happening. 'You can be such a whimsy fierce mystery, sometimes, and don't think I don't know your tricks and all.'

He's resigned to fate. Understanding he is bested again and is copping a scolding. Hearing, *Robin, you can't control everything.*

He takes Rose in his arms urgently, frantic now, knowing he is about to lose her. 'I will find you. I have waited through eternity inside your dreams. But with this tolling swift and strong and in a moment you'll be gone without memory of here. But I swear it, that in every time and within every world I'll seek you. I love you Rose. I *will* find you.'

He holds her as though someone's life depends on it. As it probably does.

At the entrance to the alley, in the dark of the storm-threatening night the first siren is quickly followed by another.

Rose squats, dazed and trembling with both outrage and cold, beside her father, black blood pooling across his face and down into the storm drain.

The piercing of the sirens is in stark juxtaposition to the strangely peaceful look on Ailín's frozen face.

Two ambulances and two police cars arrive within minutes of each other. Paramedics in blue coveralls, gloves and disposable shoe protection, carry a *LifePak*, to her father's body, leaving the red and blue emergency lights to eerie-up the night, floodies illuminating the scene.

One observes the screen for signs of life and checks Ailín for a pulse. A light is shone into his wide open eyes, and she declares, 'pupils fixed and dilated.' While another wraps Rose in a thermal blanket, takes her vitals and speaks softly to her about the grueling procedure ahead of her.

Police secure the scene and detail the situation into coms. Information is exchanged between responders, and while one of the freed-up vehicles leaves on another call-out someone from the second truck brings Rose a bottle of water and a cardboard cup of hot coffee. 'Is there anyone I can call to come wait with you? You're in for a long night.'

Rose fumbles with her phone and brings up Sam's name in her contacts. She hands the phone over.

'Hi Sam? This is Patty Allen. I'm a paramedic with New Rathmore Central Emergency, and I'm here with Rose Wen. No, she's okay, it's her dad. Yes, she'll be at the ambulance. Thanks, it's appreciated.'

She connects to Google maps and sends him the link. She hands back the phone before helping Rose to their vehicle at the entrance to the alley. The crime squad will want her out of their way.

She's settled on the back dashboard of the open ambulance when one of the police officers joins her. 'Ms.?'

Rose's voice cracks. 'Rose Wen. He's my dad. Oh, god. Who'd do such a thing. He's an old fool but he wouldn't hurt anyone.'

'I'm so sorry for your loss. Homicide and forensics are on the way. Shouldn't be too long.'

Within ten minutes a plain car pulls up and Detective Inspector John Lannard, a black man about fifty with a strong face, half obscured by an old, brown, wool beanie maneuvers himself from the driver's side. Big bodied, but with a tiredness to him that comes from seeing and knowing the things no one should ever have to see and know, he is accompanied by a younger man, the look of a raptor about him, in jeans and a bulky puffer jacket, the hood pulled up against the cold.

Forensics arrive, suiting up in white and gloves, one adjusting her camera. They head to Ailín's corpse while Lannard, nodding acknowledgement to the uniformed police, strides to Rose, squats beside her and shows her his identification. 'Ms. Wen, I'm Detective Inspector John Lannard, but please, call me John.'

In Police Headquarters, New Rathmore Central, John Lannard's wishing the chairs in the interview room didn't have to be so uncomfortable. He wonders, briefly, given that cops in this part of the world aren't as deprived of funds as in others, whether it is intentional on some bastard's part. He's imagining how cruel it must be on the backside of a rake of an old man like Billy Shando.

A laptop is open between him and Billy, and a police-issue camera is set up at the end of the table in preparation for the official interview. Two plain clothes officers are chilling out with coffees, scrolling through their cell phones, while one, in uniform, chats quietly with an emergency worker in dark blue coveralls, down near the window, now streaked with rain, the city beyond invisible.

Lannard turns the laptop screen towards Billy before diverting his attention to the police-issue camera. Lannard displays his ID.

'John Lannard, Detective Inspector, New Rathmore Metropolitan and Central Police Department, warrant number 21DI312070. I am authorized to conduct this interview on behalf of the City of New Rathmore and the Office of the Department of Justice of Blackwell County, under the jurisdiction of the state. This interview is with Mister William Shando of Unit four, fifteen Ellis Towers, High Street, New Rathmore, West. Thank you for your assistance, Mr. Shando.'

'Billy. My friends call me Father Bill or brother Billy sometimes.' He's sucking Fanta through a paper straw and his cheeks collapse with every pull. Lannard wonders if he's got any teeth, he certainly hasn't smiled, even once. But Lannard is here to watch and listen, not to be friendly.

'Father? Are you a priest, Billy?'

'I thought I was once. Haven't we done this before?'

Lannard ignores the question. 'Mr. Shando, were you present July fifteenth, at the Sailors Rest pub on the night Mr. Wen was allegedly murdered?'

'I was at the Sailors Rest pub on the night, so'

'And was there an altercation inside that same establishment between Mr. Wen and another man?'

'Is 'Mr. Wen' Ailín?'

'Ailín Wen, yes.'

'There was.'

The police in the room appear oblivious or uninterested. An experienced necessity. Comforting to the person on the hot seat.

'Mr. Shando. Can you describe what happened?'

Billy tells what he remembers, and Lannard continues his gravel-soft interrogation. 'Mr. Shando, were you intoxicated on the night of the alleged murder of Ailín Wen?'

'I was taken with drink, so.'

'Please look at the faces on the screen, Billy. Just scroll the image to your left to get to the next one. If you think you recognize any of the men at the table that night, or the men who verbally harassed Ailín Wen, could you say aloud: *I recognize this man.* And look into the camera as you do so.'

Billy scrolls, nervously. He stops before the image of the big man, Peter Randall, who later laid the first punch. He goes green around the mouth, scraping his whole chair sideways to both the screen and Lannard, sucking up the soda.

'Billy?'

'They all left before us. If I say anything what does it matter? My can's empty and I need a fag. Can I go now?'

'Almost done, thanks Billy. Do you recognize that man?'

'He was with them, sure.' He laughs, a quick indrawn breath of comprehension that no one else understands. 'This is déjà vu. I've dreamed this whole fecken event.'

'You're sure he was with them?'

'It wouldn't matter if he wasn't. He's not the one who spoke.'

'Note,' Lannard says, looking towards the camera, 'the witness has identified Peter Randall, record number BCC212390MD. The D is for deceased, Mr. Shando. The man you've identified is deceased.'

'I need a wee or I'll piss myself.'

Lannard indicates the camera. 'This interview is paused at 16:42 hours.'

Billy goes with the uniformed cop, reentering ten minutes later. Lannard allows everyone to settle, shuffling though physical notes.

'We right?'

The camera is restarted. Lannard checks the time. 'The interview with Mr. William Shando resumes at 16:54 hours. Right. Billy?'

Billy scrolls across image after image, pausing every now and then but saying nothing. He eventually sits back, his hands in his lap, eyes watching the screen.

'He'll send them after me if I say. If I do what you want it's my death next.'

'Who's 'he', Mr. Shando?'

Billy looks Lannard in the eye for the longest time, shifting in his chair before staring out the other window onto the big wide bustling main office, his lips a thin line of silence.

'Mr. Shando?'

'I showed you who he fecken is.'

Lannard powers down the laptop. 'Mr. Shando, do you have anything to add?'

Billy turns the screen in his direction, looking at his own dark reflection. 'He looks like me,' he whispers. Did you notice that about the man you say is dead? What's his name?'

'He looks nothing like you, Mr. Shando. Also, we may need to call on you again, so don't you disappear on me. Officer Stanley will drive you back to your flat.'

John couldn't have explained to anyone why Billy Shando's final comments unnerved him as much as they did.

...

8

OF HORSEHAIR TINGS AND GOLDEN RINGS

IN A SEA OF BLACK UMBRELLAS, THE misting rain mixes with people's breath. Rose stands alongside Sam at the open grave, the only woman amongst mourners. She holds a generic bouquet of supermarket flowers, in green tissue paper and cellophane, in one hand, an open umbrella in the other. The barman and other men from Ailín's pub shelter under the makeshift plastic gazebo as the downpour becomes a wall of wet grey. Billy Shando keeps himself separate from the others, his head downcast, his collar up, rain running from the brim of his flaccid felt hat as though from a downpipe.

The lay celebrant is a tall woman, dressed in white, her hair crowned in tiny ferns and small flowers. She holds her own umbrella, rainbow-striped. Such a hippy thing, Rose thinks.

'Allan Wen now slumbers within the earth's embrace, remembered by his beloved daughter Rose and all those who knew him so well for his humor and his stories. May he rest in eternal peace.'

There are mumbles of *amen* and several of the men cross themselves and the celebrant smiles down at Rose.

'Ms. Wen?'

Rose ignores the question and drops the bouquet onto the coffin. She walks away and Sam joins her.

'Anytime you want to talk about my take on the spirits and stuff, I'm available,' he says, seriously, watching the slippery ground to keep his footing.

'What?'

'There's a lot of dark in you, *je vois*.'

'No offense Sam but don't you start.'

'None taken. Can I buy you coffee?'

She pauses by the roadside and considers what is to happen next. She sees nothing, feels nothing. There's endlessness in the world for her to do today. And even tomorrow, if she doesn't make it otherwise. 'Yes, I'd like that,' she replies distractedly.

Before she and Sam cross the road to his car, Billy Shando shambles to her, head down, his hat shadowing the top half of his face. He raises his eyes, blinking as rain lands on his eyelashes.

'Róisín, sorry to interrupt.'

'Hi. Thank you for coming. Did you know my father?'

'Billy Shando is my name. We come over on the ship together. I knew you when you were little.'

'You're wet, Billy Shando, and I don't remember you at all.'

'I thought you should know where to come, so. Here——'

He pulls a folded slip of paper from his pocket and offers it to her.

'I'll be somewhere down around Limerick.' His voice trails off, thinking the gesture useless.

Rose stows the note into her bag. 'I'm sorry for your loss, Mr. Shando.'

She and Sam navigate the traffic, leaving Billy forlorn and alone amongst gravestones. He should be confused by the way she says what she does, but he's not. The rain pelts down but now he's oblivious to its demand. *Dear Mother Mercy*, he thinks, *what else does you want from me?*

In the rundown diner nineties elevator music gives the place an ambience of being shallow and crass. Rose toys with her spoon and Sam just watches. Knowing. Patient.

'I'm glad you called me.' He stretches the cramps from his fingers. 'It's hard losing family. What now?'

Rose, lets out the breath she hadn't been aware she'd been holding. 'I don't know, yet. I'm not going to live in his house, that's for sure. I'll get my things out today.'

'You need a place to stay?'

'I'm staying in a hotel till I work out details. Until I sell the house. If I can, that is. It's a dump, Sam.'

'*Bien.* You're welcome to camp on my sofa. Janet really likes you.'

'Thanks Sam, and thank Janet for me too, but I have to be on my own.' Rose shoulders her bag.

He shoves his frozen hands deep into the pockets of his coat and quietly reminds her, '*In the darkness lay a secret she'd forgotten for so long, and as she removes it gently from its deep she hums to it her own song. The humming builds, becoming words burning with intent, and she stumbles, startled, having thought her forever song long spent.*'

Rose is not following his behavior at all today, between poetry, French and spirits, he almost seems like a stranger. 'Whose work?'

'Yours.'

Then it hits her. 'Is that—'

'The writing you didn't think I'd like. Your term paper.'

His eyes follow her, full of sadness, before he kisses her forehead.

'Do you need a ride?'

She's stiff, wondering if he's making a pass. She really cannot read body language. Never could. 'No. Thanks. I'm fine.'

He sighs, missing none of the implications that scud through her thoughts, reading her with the practice of a tracker understanding wolf scat. 'Just remember some people are actually your friends and you can't keep this up forever without something very bad happening, *d'accord*?'

He walks out and Rose is left perplexed.

At 64 Lafayette Street the taxi pulls up and Rose pays the driver. She stands in the gloom on the sidewalk and watches the house as if waiting for it to say something.

She cajoles open the objecting, rust-hinged old gate, goes up the pebble path to the front door, and lets herself into the house, switching on the light, glad she forgot to have the electricity disconnected. She hasn't been here since the night Ailín died. Why then, is she surprised that everything is so unfamiliar? That the police have left it even neater than when she and her father lived here. It seems smaller somehow.

She jostles two suitcases from the closet in her bedroom and dumps them, open, on the bed. She throws in clothes and a few possessions, forces the luggage shut and drags it to beside the front door.

She is motionless, her head bent, nothing readable about her face. She forces herself to go into her father's room.

His bed is unmade, his dressing gown and pajamas thrown on it carelessly. *Like him*, she thinks.

The only other furniture is an old wardrobe and a mirrored dresser on which is a half-empty bottle of Laphroaig single malt, an overfull ashtray and a pair of tattered gardening gloves. 'Where's me, huh, Dad?'

She opens the top dresser drawer and moves things around. She repeats this with the other drawers becoming angrier as she strews the contents onto the floor.

'Not one. Not even one fucking photograph.'

Her attention is drawn to the wardrobe. She pulls savagely at the stuck doors. A few clothes hang on wire hangers and dirt-crusted Wellington boots are on the floor of the cupboard. A hand-crafted wooden box the size of a small milk crate, with RÓISÍN carved into the lid, is pushed into one corner. She frowns, and pulls it out.

She picks it up, it's light enough. She carries it to the sitting room.

She switches the four-bar heater to full and sits on the threadbare rug shivering with both cold and trepidation.

Within, on the very top, is a small, framed photograph of her mother with a baby in her arms. Ailín, young, stands proudly beside them, in front of their vardo.

A dozen more sepia photos scatter beneath her hands, some of Rose when she was a girl and of some other people. Rose studies each one, thinking, perhaps, she recognizes Billy Shando, but the image is too faded to be sure. Trying to make sense of these smiling unrecognizable faces.

A layer of tea towels hides several more things including an envelope with her name on it. Rose unseals it, unfolds the brittle paper and reads, between picking out the other contents of the box.

My darling Róisín, I'm dead now because I know you won't come into my room unless that is the case. I'm sorry.

A bangle made of white horsehair, ornately bound and beaded with talismans and amulets, red thread, small bones and human hair woven through with small gold beads and glowing with amber-like resin. *I tried but I couldn't. I miss your mother to this very day and the hurt won't let go.*

A thin, tight plaited length of more hair, the three colors of her and her parents: hers light red, her father's the brown of dark chocolate, her mother's as black as raven's wings, the last making her eyes sting with the memory of the woman he loved more than life. The braid is tied at both ends with ribbon and, underneath where it has laid for who knows how long, is a tattered book of Yeats poetry, minus the cover, bearing a handwritten homage on the title page: Love beyond all else, yours always, xxx. *I love you so much, but I know you're ashamed of me so I'm sorry again.*

A scratched gold signet ring with a rampant horse carved into it, set with an emerald, that would have fitted her own hand more than any man's. A fleeting thought, soon forgotten. A pretty shoe she does remember. For the red glitter. How old had she been then? Three?

I've always been sorry, a cara. *You're the light left in my darkness after Orla.*

Rose pauses reading, almost loses the hard-won steely hold over her emotions. *Now if you don't want to do what I've to ask I'll understand but I'd be happy to not have my spirit lost as well, so.*

The soft, russet pelt, light fur and dark, of some long-dead animal. *If the money's enough and you feel it in your heart to do it will you take my things back to the woods...*

A wad of cash is held together with an elastic band, with an address hand printed on a scrap of paper *...and burn them where our vardo went up in flames, sending your mother to Tir na n'Óg all the years gone since.*

Rose's jaw clenches and releases, her head aching because she can't seem to stop. *Will you take the road? Here's the last known address of the man closest thing to a brother I ever had, Gyf—Gyofan Borran— where he settled after the Garda chased us off. It's him will know what's to be done.*

'No Dad, I won't.' She folds the paper and replaces it, the book, the photographs and the peculiarity of all the other objects back inside. She closes the lid and lays the box with her luggage, keying the cab company number into her cell phone.

...

9

HUNTER RAT AND THE WATCHING WIND
The Storyteller's First Interruption

IT'S ME AGAIN. SHELDRÚ. I'm to tell you of her lost days, see, because the season passes, it's sad to say, one year round, like a circle in a circle, like a wheel within a wheel… who said that? Doesn't matter now. I've forgotten more things, and people's names, than most will ever know.

I'm that stupid-looking pigeon among pigeons, with my silly head going back and forth, back and forth, pecking at bits of rubbishy food-droppings off the ground, the scraps of the untidy, and pretending to care. I'm at the school, see. Rathmore West High School. On a grey forgettable day. Róisín's moving, hypnotical-like, through a crowd, none of whom notice her or pay her any mind. She goes up the steps and through the security checkpoint, clumsy despite how hard she tries to be otherwise, scattering her paperwork. Almost dropping her laptop.

I watch her through the eyes of a hunter rat patrolling the window-ledge outside her hotel room, on one particularly sleepless night. She sits up in bed, realizing that dawn'll soon obscure the city lights outside her window, possibly seeing me, probably not caring, what with the glass between us and me so quick on me feet still, even though I am old. I see her reaching, exasperated with this incessant wakefulness, to switch off the lamp, her eyes briefly alighting on my son's wooden box in the corner of the room.

A year or so later and I'm a proud north wind, flowing about a college before drafting through the lecture hall. And there she is, at an unsociable distance from the other students, her professor droning on like an eejit about John Donne, a sixteenth century Catholic feller, whose work is highly forgettable, mind, and who's name, therefore, should not be mentioned, other than as a footnote, in any decent text. The lecturer's voice, as a result, dos not register one iota, and if he'd kept on she would at least have had a decent sleep.

Me, however, I'm thinking concentrate, concentrate, she's why you stayed in the land of men, you old púca now, yourself, so, *while she catches herself and takes notes.*

In a moment of contrariness, late on the eve of midsummer when it's still light enough to see, she visits 64 Lafayette Street but won't go in.

Some inexplicable nostalgia to visit the rowan tree and climb the frond-and-berry-burgeoning branches, high enough to be looking down on the kitchen window below, the now rusted awning allows her speckled glimpses of the sink, and the laminate-topped bench curling at the edge where the damp and rot have got in. I recall that our rowan tree was the only thing she dared climb all through her years as a leanbh—*child. Not out of fear of falling, understand, but from the sure realization that if she reached too great a height, on anything without branches in which she could hide, someone would see her, and they were sure to tell Ailín. And she'd get some story that would last for hours, with a moral at the end, that she was better without.*

She knew, although he never said, that he was terrified of something hurting to her. Of losing her too. As irrational as it seemed she was sure it was a memory the tree tells her. Then she climbs down. All sensible. And has an unbidden thought that the back garden, so neglected and overgrown with weeds, is even more beautiful for the wildness of it somehow (a touch of me in her, I now realize), the flowers amongst it, the thyme and the sage thick with scent, the roses going to head without a-nipping, the hips round and pregnant with seeds, strong.

Her rowan tree, dear rowan tree, in full leaf, heavy with bright, blood red berries. On the city street, packed with mindless commuters, I'm madly-blown detritus, caught up in some seasonlessness, neither hot-nor-cold bluster, as she frantically rushes to catch her bus, missing it by seconds.

And last but, by now you've probably realized, never least, when summer reaches her fullness, but before the big heat bringing with it the midges and mosquitoes like the plague, at very close to five in the morning, she closes her laptop and switches off the lamp. Her eyes adjust to that smudge of light that paints the sky just before dawn, ignoring me from where I observe, in the company of a murder of other ravens, from the vantage of the power lines; just another fecken bird amongst birds, her eyes wandering against her will to the forlorn, still-abandoned box. This time unable to look away.

Giving in to her tired enchantment, or some unheard spell, by you know who by now, she retrieves it from the floor, opens the lid and re-reads the letter. Then she picks up the wad of cash, so.

'Leave no black plume as a token of that lie thy soul hath spoken. Leave my loneliness unbroken.'

Don't think you've heard the last from me, though. I'm not all the way into Tir na n'Óg yet.

...

.

A POVERTY OF GYPSIES

AT THE SHANNON airport Rose pushes a trolley with her overstuffed backpack, hand luggage, the box in cling wrap and her laptop, out onto the street, and over to the waiting line of cabs.

The driver of the first car helps her put the lot into the boot, gets back behind the wheel and waits until she's buckled up beside him, the box on her lap.

'Where to is it today?' he asks, a thick Irish accent.

She reads from her iPhone: 'It's called Avalon House. 55 Aungier Street. A hostel.'

'Grand spot,' he says over his shoulder, 'On holidays?'

'I suppose.'

'Well Temple Bar's the place to be for the fun,' and he navigates, shark-like, into the nine kilometer traffic nightmare to get her to the hostel in one piece. When they arrive, the music in his stereo blaring, he deposits Rose's luggage on the pavement for her out front of her destination.

She taps her credit card on the charger and shakes her head when he asks if she wants a receipt. She's numb, out of her depths, assaulted by the strange sights and smells, the emotional rollercoaster turning her guts to water.

Rose shows him the address she's keyed into her phone from her father's letter. 'Can you tell me where this is, please?'

'You don't want to be going there, miss.' He is kind, like she's a child.

'Why not?'

'I don't want to sound a bigot, miss, but it's full of gypsies and they'll rob you or worse, so.' He waits for a response but there is none.

Rose shoulders her backpack, picks up her hand luggage and the box, and struggles into the hostel without looking back at him.

At the reception desk a tattooed, pierced, meticulously made up young woman at the reception desk works on the computer.

She looks up as Rose approaches, beaming. 'I'm Abbie. Can I help you?'

'Rose Wen, Abbie. I've got a booking.'

Abbie checks the records. 'Overnight, is it you're staying?'

Rose, dumps her possessions, unable to keep up the charade that she's juggling it all. 'I'm not sure yet,' she says.

Abbie lays a standard form on the counter and hands across a pen.

'Can you fill this out please, Rose?'

Rose does so, and Abbie photocopies it and registers her passport and credit card details before handing across a room access card. 'You're on the ground floor and the kitchen facility is available all day and all night. Although there's usually a crowd but they're lovely. Laundry is at the rear of the building. Rubbish to be recycled. Any questions feel free.'

Rose thanks her and picks up her bags and the box. Abbie laughs and gestures her mouth, putting the key card between her guest's teeth,' adding, cryptically, 'Hope you find what you came for.'

Rose finally gets the lock open, not used to the synchronization necessary for everything to work, Inside, she is oblivious to her surroundings, not caring. She's got the room to herself unlike the majority of hostels. Worth the extra Euros.

She dumps her luggage and cracks open a large paper shopping bag into which she slides the box. She opens her laptop to Google maps and sits on the edge of the bed just staring at the screen for what feels like hours.

Adjacent to a slum of tower flats and neglect, Rose steps down off the bus with the box in the shopping bag, her purse slung over her shoulder to protect it just in case. She takes in the squalor, rubbish, old cars and concrete, thinking of how like it is to Lafayette Street, just with high rise decrepitude and abandonment instead of clapboard single-frontage council houses.

She targets a group of youth kicking a soccer ball across the quadrangle and approaches the clique of thin-lipped, spotty-faced, seen everything teenagers who yell at the players from the sidelines and share music from joint earbuds.

She hands around the note of the name and address. A girl points to a cinder block-and-concrete steel tower of flats, each with tiny windows, like upright, blind coffins.

Inside, the walls that were cream once upon a time are now obscured by tagging and concrete rust, the stench of spray can paint, old wine, something rotten and dried urine overwhelming. Rose pushes the *up* button on the steel-doored elevator and waits.

On the ninth floor she walks the dimly lit corridor, her shoes squelching on linoleum. She comes to 912 and knocks.

The door is opened by a big-breasted woman somewhere in her forties, worn and tired, her hair bleached to an unfortunate shade of yellow, a rosary disappearing into her cleavage and bangles from wrist to elbow.

'If you're a Jehovah's Witness that lost her fecken partner to sin we don't care, you can just feck off now because we don't care, I'm a good Catholic—' Deirdra Borran makes a strangled sound deep in her throat and sticks her chin out looking like she could take on a gorilla in an unfair fight. 'and I don't care.'

'Sorry.' Rose isn't, but it seems appropriate. 'Does Gyofan Borran live here?'

'Who's asking for me, Deirdra?' booms a massive voice from inside.

'What do you want with him, and who the bejesus are you?'

'I'm Rose Wen and you can stop speaking to me like that because— you see—I also don't care who you are, either.'

The door is yanked wide and Gyofan Borran, a year maybe two

younger than her father, pulls it all the way open, almost unhinging it. He stares, open-mouthed. He has a magnificent moustache and a full head of almost-black hair. Bull-chested, over six feet tall, wearing workman's pants and a red and yellow paisley satin waistcoat over a sweat-stained cotton singlet, a brightly colored kerchief around his throat. Heavy silver earrings are in both ears and a string of turquoise beads adorns his neck.

'You're fecken gorgeous, Róisín!' He grabs her in a bear hug and half-carries her into a squalid main room.

Sitting watching television are Síon, seventeen years old, eldritch in an untamed way. Bleached, ice-white hair smoothed and straightened. Makeup that's been well-studied in tutorials and practiced amongst her friends, silver hoop earrings almost to her shoulders. Four young men aged from early to late teens are crammed beside her on the sofa and Sheldrú, a weather-skinned woman in her sixties, has long grey hair in braids to her waist, her body heavy with jewelry and talismans.

She is Gyofan's mother and, although lined and weary, she is straight backed and her eyes are an intense, scrutinizing ice-blue, oddly young against the leather of her exposed skin.

Gyofan puts Rose down and stands back to observe her.

'Sheldrú, this is Ailín's Rose.' He seems to shout but Rose soon understands that this is his normal voice. 'Mam, will you look at her? She's the image of her mother but with fire on the hill. I forgot about that hair, Róisín.'

Sheldrú rises, wincing, from the couch and comes face to face with Rose. 'He's died then, is it so?'

'Who're you talking about, you two?' Deirdra, is acerbic still. 'And do you mind telling me what's going on in my own home?'

'Ailín Wen's Róisín,' says Gyofan. 'Róisín, Deirdra's my wife and she's got a heart of gold. Sometimes. Don't let her scare you. She says what she says out of caution. He's died, am I right?' Rose nods.

The younger people pay no attention but Gyofan, moving with lithe grace for a man of his size, clears stuff from a table and seats Rose on one of the chairs there.

'Where's manners, wife? We've a guest requiring hospitality,' Sheldrú hisses, glaring at Deirdra with distaste.

Deirdra huffs off into the kitchen just off the main room, closed out, as sometimes happens when certain things within a family are not peculiar outside of the blood, try and understand as they might.

Rose puts her shopping bag on the table and removes the box.

'What is it you have here, Róisín?' asks Sheldrú, kindly.

Rose opens the lid and takes out the letter, reading the last part as Gyofan and Sheldrú peer in at the contents.

Rose reads. *Will you take the road? Here's the last known address of the man closest thing to a brother I ever had, Gyofan Borran.*

She slides the letter back in the box as Deirdra returns with a tray of tea and biscuits, landing them gracelessly in the middle of the table.

Gyofan picks up the ring, a resigned look to his eyes, his eyebrows steepling in the center of his forehead with a grief she doesn't, herself, feel. 'I have to hang onto this for a while,' he explains, pocketing the ring.

Rose examines her fingers where the marks from the box's edge have gouged into them. 'Keep it, I don't care.'

'Sure, it's not mine to keep,' he assures her, 'but it's not your father's either.'

Rose lifts her face to his, certain of its studied apathy. But that's not what the gypsy sees, nor his mother. Gyofan and Sheldrú glance at each other knowingly, inscrutably. Each comprehends what the other does. Her eyes. A moss green pair of cutthroat razors that Ailín's daughter is oblivious to, speaking with more so than her voice ever could.

'I don't understand.'

Gyofan recognizes the rage for what it is. The desperation of isolation. The not belonging. The crushing loneliness of someone devoid of their kindred and clan. The hurt. The hidden wild creature.

'You will, I promise, so,' he assures her, his voice gentling her as though she is one of his horses.

Rose takes a mug of tea, mixes in milk and a spoon of sugar, leaving in the bag. She observes Sheldrú across the table as the old woman clutches at Gyofan's sleeve, appearing as though she's maybe having a stroke because her eyes have glazed over and have rolled up slightly, exposing only the whites.

'Shite. Here we go,' sighs Deirdra, counting. '*hain, dough tree, caher, coig*—' one, two three four, five, she counts in Irish, before Sheldrú's gaze clears and she shoots a look of derision at Deirdra that should have killed her where she stood. Then she drags her gaze away and nods at her son.

'It's all safe. No Garda. And it's very important to do this thing he wants. Or his ghost won't stay dead.' To Deirdra, he says, 'he'll be lost, *a cara*. So.'

There is no question in his mind. Nothing to consider. 'We're for the road.'

Rose is bewildered by the uncanny experience, but Gyofan pats her gently on the shoulder, smiling, all charm.

'What just happened?' she asks, curiosity about the ways of people who are probably her own kind softening her resolve to caution.

'Old woman's got the gift,' says the big man, defying council house rules and rolling himself a cigarette. Lighting it and opening the window to blow the smoke away.

'But we don't talk about it,' Sheldrú advises. 'It upsets the religious.'

'The gift of?'

'The sight, Róisín. Seeing things before they happen.' Sheldrú shifts on her chair, taking up a cup of the tea for herself. 'Healing and cursing and the like. A gift we don't take light, like, either.'

Rose tries to digest this but Deirdra is outraged. 'We're not going anywhere. And I don't believe in ghosts, so. Are you gone daft?' She turns on Rose. 'What're you doing coming here fecken things up.'

Gyofan, outraged, says, 'Don't speak to the old king's daughter like that. Not ever.'

'The what?' Rose asks, her voice catching in her throat.

'Where's your things Róisín? You'll stay with us till it's sorted.' Sheldrú holds out her hand and one of the boys drops a cell phone into it as though she'd asked. Her thumbs text like she's done it forever.

Rose scans the squalor. 'I've got a place.'

'Nonsense.' Gyofan restocks the box, methodically and reverently.

'Síon'll sleep in with me,' Sheldrú says, matter of factually. 'It's the way of things, Róisín. Gyofan, get your lad Ruairí's van. Go with her for her stuff. I've just let him know you're on the way.'

Síon, her body lean and toned like a dancer, or a fighter, her breasts perhaps real, perhaps not, gets up from the couch adjusting her iPod, her earbuds in her ears, and a can of Red Bull in her hand, a grin a mile wide.

'I'm Síon, and I'm Gyofan Borran's only girl, so I get a room to myself, like Mamó.' She gestures to Sheldrú, using the Irish familiarity for grandmother. 'And you can bunk in with me, sure, but Mamó, I'll not share a bed.'

Rose begins to protest again but Sheldrú places her finger to her own lips in a gesture for silence. And like a spell is cast, Rose has nothing to say.

Gyofan calls to the boys and takes Rose by the hand. 'The box will be safe here if you're alright to trust it to my matháir.'

Deirdra turns on Sheldrú, hoping no one else can hear. 'You'll put us all in the shite you fecken nasty old woman.'

'You'll shut up and remember who I am and what I can do.' Sheldrú pins her braids on top of her head, a gesture of readiness for a fight not lost on Deirdra. 'You're not invited anyway.'

They face off but it's a no contest. Deirdra's eyes drop, decidedly nervous.

That night, out on the quadrangle, all the gypsies from all the clans now living in Dublin and in the neighborhood are gathered by a fire ablaze in a forty-four-gallon drum. Children and teenagers of all ages kick at soccer balls on the cracked concrete oblivious to the meaning of the coming together.

An accordion player, a fiddler, a woman with a tin whistle and two people on guitars fill the summer twilight with a tune, while the old and the young dance and pass porter, poteen and pipes of sweet smelling smoke that has nothing of tobacco in it, from one to the other.

Deirdra and a small cabal of women huddle together, stony-faced and disagreeable.

Rose is seated at on a wooden fruit box beside Sheldrú, Gyofan and Síon. So is Billy Shando, to Rose's confusion. He is dressed in trousers and suspenders. The grey hat is now adorned with cockerel feathers in the ribbon and it's shoved down over thick, curly, long blondish, greying hair. He no longer looks like a rough sleeper in thrift shop sweatpants and worn out sneakers, replaced, instead, by sturdy boots that lace up with strong cord. His hands surround a small glass jar with the gold of whisky three fingers deep. The men form a circle, speaking in hushed discussion, in a language Rose only vaguely recalls her father speaking sometimes.

Gyofan stretches, before striding to the heart of the gathering, his arms wide and his head bent, waiting for silence.

He gestures to Rose who comes and stands with him.

'So I suppose you've all learned,' he booms with that voice she first heard in the hallway, 'but in case you don't know, this here's Róisín Wen, daughter of Ailín Wen, also known as Ailín rí, the last king of our own, who is now dead. Buried because he was lost and made no vardo after his love went before him. And that means two things. First it means we got to decide who's next to carry that responsibility.'

Some silly young lad, all hormones and bravado shouts loud enough for everyone to hear. 'As if that matters anymore.'

Gyofan, his face pale, his fists clenched like legs of ham, turns on his heel and storms right up to the lad who clusters for safety behind others.

'While I live and breathe it matters, you wee shite of a *gowl*.'

The young men the boy is hiding behind part. They don't agree with him because, in truth, there's not a one of them doesn't hate this place and this way of life. So whatever happens, happens. He's called this onto himself with the disrespect of the uninitiated. A kid who's never known the life.

'We might have got kicked off the roads, but we're still fecken-well alive so don't let me hear that disrespect coming out of you ever again, am I understood?'

The youth lowers his face, the whole scenario registering; the behavior of the others turning his guts to acid. He is ashamed and he'll wait for someone to tell him why. Probably still get a beating anyway.

Gyofan returns to the center of the gathering and looks to Sheldrú and the others of the inner circle, his eyes like mist in the lightlessness of the polluted night, despite the fire. 'So who's it to be?'

Billy Shando might look old and worn out to the bone but when he speaks his voice is clear and rich, the fear that held him captive at both the pub and in the police headquarters, gone. Replaced by someone John Lannard would not have recognized.

'We all remember Róisín and the sadness with her *máthair* dying like she did,' he says, 'and how Gyofan Borran and Sheldrú helped Ailín, and stood by the rest of us all through the Settlement. So it's to be our man, Gyofan Borran. Might as well. You being Ailín rí's brother in all but blood, and him leaving the way he did, poor man, may this be a settling for his wandering soul. Who agrees?'

There is assent from a hundred or more tempered voices, with language and accents that Rose doesn't understand. So very confused by events. 'I don't remember. I don't remember anyone Were they—'

'All there when it happened?' says Gyofan softly. 'So.'

'Do you have it?' Billy asks, his tone serious, at odds with his smiling face.

Gyofan takes the ring from his pocket and hands it to Billy Shando who holds it aloft. 'Sheldrú?'

There's clapping and ruckus, alongside dissatisfied mumbles from the boundary of the circle, as Sheldrú takes the ring.

She spits on it and walks around the circle so that everyone gets to have a look. Then she goes to Gyofan and unsmiling, forces it over the first knuckle of his little finger. She slaps his face saying, 'You mind how you go, now.'

Billy Shando sighs, and holds his jar of whisky high. 'Raise your glasses. All luck to you, Gyofan Borran also now known as Gyofan rí.'

'All luck to the king!'

Mumbles, cheers and apathetic grunts from the stoned and half-drunk gathering.

Sheldrú returns to her seat, a dark and broody frown turning down the corners of her mouth. Gyofan lifts his hand, demanding quiet. 'So, to the second thing is that it's the dying wish of our man that if the fates are with us, and also Róisín, we take to the roads to see him off with Orla. And I'm already going.'

There is much approval but equal dissent, especially amongst the women. Deirdra and her friends leave pointedly. Gyofan's sons, in defiance of doubt, stand with their father. Síon observes Rose intently as the music starts up again.

...

11

POOK

TWILIGHT IS LONG IN IRELAND'S summer and the convoy of several old cars, some with trailers, trundle dusty, less-traveled country roads, through the hours of dusky light.

Gyofan drives a big old 1972 Bedford bus that's been gutted on the inside, transformed into living quarters, complete with a wood stove and an enamel bathtub that hangs from the rear wall like the Hunchback of Notre Dame. Rose is crammed into the seat up front, squashed between Sheldrú and Síon.

The convoy travel the Connemara back roads and make their first camp down the end of a tractor trail, amidst the lush landscape of rivulets and lakes, in sight of the *pins*, on the move the next day and the day after that.

Rose joins in with the chores, the setting up in the evening and the dismantling at dawn and at each encampment she gains confidence, relaxing in a way she is unused to, living in the city. Happy at the growing familiarity.

Off to their right, along the sea road, are views of the dark foam-flecked water and the staggering geology of the cliffs of the west coast. They travel south from Galway, via Kilrush through Ballybunnion and from there Tralee, Dingle, Killorgen, Kenmare by way of Kinsale and past Carrigaline. To the outskirts of Cork near the hills where the Fenian warriors kept a lookout, once upon a time in the dark days of an oral history.

In the dense, wild, primordial forest that the English never cut down for their castles, cathedrals and ships, a mere stone's throw from the ancient roundhouse tower, the camp is set up in the clearing only known to them, down a bramble and wild gorse, heather and strawberry-lined disused cattle track.

Several of the men bristle, prepared for trouble and reaching for weapons as Robin, on his deep-rumbling motorcycle, rides into sight. Gyofan unsheathes a knife from his belt but is held back by Billy Shando. Sheldrú strides knowingly to Robin, who struggles out of his old leather jacket but remains astride the bike, picking at loose threads around the collar as though he is alone and the unpicking is important.

When she's almost upon him he looks up, reading her. He dismounts, turning off the ignition, leaning the vehicle on its kickstand, removing his helmet and shaking out his hair. He holds it back with a hair tie from around his wrist. He smiles at Sheldrú, the forthrightness in the look lighting his dark eyes with an intimacy that no one watching would understand. She takes his hands.

'Old woman,' he says, but kindly.

'You here for a reason?'

'Is there a craic to be had?'

'Ailín Wen's died,' she tells him, aware he already probably knows. Wondering if he might not have had a hand in it somehow, aware enough about the fáidh to remember that their ideas of right and wrong don't gel with expectations of a tame species.

He shrugs. It's a kind of yes.

'You going to be a problem?' She asks this while her fingers move a stray raggedy lock of his hair to behind one ear. Something intimate about the gesture. Or something a mother would do for her child.

Robin drops his jacket over the worn seat, loose threads forgotten, grinning, a ready quote from Shakespeare his reply. '*If we shadows have offended...*'

Sheldrú slugs his shoulder. 'Be quiet now.'

'You going to introduce me?'

She leads Robin to the campsite.

'Well?' Gyofan is still cautious, re-sheathing his weapon. If his mother speaks for this stranger, who is he to challenge?

'He's Robin,' she smiles, her son reading well enough the meaning. 'And he lives around here, don't you, Robin? This is his place, Gyof. I knew him when he was younger.' To the wary men she explains, 'He's alright, lads.'

Robin, his hands in his pockets, notices the gold ring with the emerald and the rampant horse on Gyofan's little finger. He queries Sheldrú. 'Where'd he get that?'

'My son, Gyofan Borran. He's the rí now.'

'If you believe it, so?' suggests Robin, hinting at more but saying nothing else, shifting his stance, before looking the big man in the eye. Gyofan returns the appraisal, like a bull in a challenge. and Robin shrugs and grins, charming the threat from the situation and shaking Gyofan's hand, grip measuring grip, and Gyofan without knowing why, has to prevent himself from bowing. Billy Shando tries to keep out of sight but there's no hiding. Never was.

'Shando?' Robin's tone insinuates something, but it's not always easy to know what the Fair Folk intend with their words.

Billy turns pale as milk, not another thing coming out of his mouth. Why bother? He's dismissed as Robin turns his attention away, more immediate concerns on his mind. 'Anyone need a hand?'

Rose has been helping Síon and Ruairí attach a canvas annex to the Bedford through all this. Robin saunters over, his hand brushing Rose's.

Síon steps between them, flirty. He's initially friendly but then attempts to ignore her; her becoming angrier and angrier. She's the daughter of the newly-declared gypsy king. To be ignored is worse than any crime as far as she's concerned, the only crueler ones being banishment or being sent to the nuns.

Come early twilight a fire is built, soon roaring within a circle of stones. A cooking grate is laid across it when it relaxes to glowing coals. The women prepare food, the men and boys bring chairs, instruments, poteen and other intoxicants from inside their vehicles, and everyone settles for the night, with some of the younger ones vanishing into the unseeing, non-judgmental forest, their own indulgences and desires drawing them into illicit, taboo, even dangerous liaisons away from protocols and tradition.

Rose is hunkered down on a large flat rock a little apart from the others and drinks tea from a cracked mug with a photo of Freddy Mercury on one half, a crown on the other.

Robin squats beside her and holds out a hand. Rose shakes it, Sheldrú watching from a distance.

'Name's Robin.'

'I'm Rose,' she says, trying to not be affected by the touch while, simultaneously fascinated at her body's unexpected reaction.

'Sheldrú said. How was the funeral?'

'What?'

'Your daddy.'

Rose appraises him blankly. 'How is any of this your business?'

'Well. I suppose it isn't. But you're on my land.'

'This?' Rose is confused. Does he mean all of it?

'Your family's vardo is dust here somewhere,' he says casually. 'Your mother's and her mother's, also.' He returns his eyes to her, the gaze trapping her. 'On my land.'

'Oh, I'm sorry. No one said.'

Robin, such a smartass, says, 'They won't. It's a pact, so. And it's not good manners to say sorry when it's not true.'

'It is true.'

'No, it is not.'

Rose despises being corrected, or actually even criticized, especially by a stranger and especially by a man. It is in her psychological makeup, now, to bristle and go on the defensive. She, of course, blames her father and the bigotry she experienced at having grown up poor and female on a street like Lafayette and in a suburb like Rathmore west. 'You must have been very young the last time we were here. You've got a good memory. You knew Sheldrú how long ago?'

'I was, and I have, and I remember your father, and not everything is everybody's business, Rose, like you said.'

Rose is mesmerized and darkly attracted to his attitude as though his words cut through what she knows as political correctness, or even just stupidity. Of course no one has to justify themselves or disclose their lives for the opinion of others. She doesn't. Not ever. So there's interest in the conversation. But she won't show it, what she's feeling, the excitement at word games that require an honesty she's unused to. 'I'm just here to finish things with him.'

'You're angry. Your voice and your face are both talking.'

Rose stands and walks away.

Robin goes to follow but Síon waylays him. She's dressed to seduce, as much as being on the road allows. 'Don't be bothered with her majesty, you'll get nowhere. Are you hanging about a while?'

He doesn't answer, deep in thought.

'Dance with me.' She takes his arm, but Robin disengages it, returning to the here and now and an out-of-the-blue uncomfortable situation that he must diffuse.

'You're fair and lovely, so. But I fear not old enough for the likes of me, and I'll not get into trouble with your daddy.'

'He won't mind.' She tries again but his eyes are those of an unpredictable wild animal, the pupils huge and black, obscuring any light, and for a moment she's fearful. She backs away from him. He brushes past her and strides off into the tower.

Síon stalks back to the fire and sits, creaking on a fold out camp chair near the other girls, feigning a pout and a look that she's practiced many times. But in truth she's pissed off and her eyes lock on Rose across the fire. Rose smiles but Síon does not.

Sheldrú rises effortlessly from her stool and follows Robin inside the ancient stone structure. The interior of the roundhouse tower is like a vast, circular chimney with internal and external stairs open to the sky.

There are no longer any upper floors because the wood rotted away centuries ago but it's obvious where they were by the regular protrusions of rock. The internal dimensions are a hundred feet across, and pigeons flutter and roost in the upper reaches while brambles and ivy, growing thick through chinks at the base hide field mice, stoats, and other small things from the unseen threat of owl or hawk.

Moss and lichen cover mortared stone. Sheldrú stands, entranced by her memories, like specters neither in her mind nor in the air around her, in the center of the space. She turns in revolutions, her arms helicoptering wide with familiarity and delight.

'Robin?' she calls to the open space.

He climbs down from high up on the ledge of one of the narrow windows, and is encircled by those arms. Drawn into her embrace.

He takes two steps back, drinking in the look of her, seeing only the lover of that wild embrace, the mother of his almost-mortal child, now grown to be a man. Now king of these gypsies.

'You are dazzling, *cailín*.'

'Don't be daft,' Sheldrú drops her gaze, embarrassed by how old she feels beside his beautiful alienness, but Robin puts a finger beneath her chin and tilts her face towards him.

'Oh, Sheldrú, *how many loved your moments of glad grace, and loved your beauty with love false or true, but one man loved the pilgrim soul in you, and loved the sorrows of your changing face.*'

Sheldrú shifts her position, her knees complaining, her pain increasing, a slight smile lighting her sad, incorrigible eyes. 'It's Róisín now?'

'It is,' he answers matter-of-factly, her knowing the nature of a the faerie as she does. 'Will things stand still long enough, do you think, for it to happen? I tried already but things went crazy. Look for me?'

'I don't need the sight to know, *mo chroi*. She's already in love,' and she sighs. Robin kisses her lightly on the lips. 'Sometimes I wish the magic would go in a straight line, just long enough for fate to make things simple.'

'If wishes were horses,' Sheldrú chuckles. 'I'm dying, Robin.'

Her announcement doesn't immediately register, but then his eyes widen with sadness and anguish, tears pricking his eyes like needles, and he can't help himself, because it's happened so many times before and he never gets used to it. He weeps silently for a long time, just letting those tears and that snot fall, heedless, and she holds him, not caring that he'll soil her best red jumper.

'Do you think that maybe once, in the long ago the faeries offended God?' she says after what feels like forever with him in her embrace.

He laughs. She feels it in her belly where once his baby had quickened.

'What god would that be?' wiping his nose on his sleeve after realizing the mess he's made. 'Sorry.'

She laughs, knowing it's not true.

'Oh, and our granddaughter's flirting with me.'

'I'll take care of Síon. Don't worry.' She leaves him alone, with ghosts of his own.

Back by the fire and Síon hasn't gone with the others to the forest. *Good girl, yourself*, Sheldrú thinks, as she grabs her granddaughter by the arm and hauls her to her feet. 'Walk a bit with me.' Her smile seems innocent and some parody of old-lady-like does not do what she intends.

'What? Why?'

Sheldrú doesn't answer but leads the girl from the others, down the slight rise to the brook.

She sits, her body aching. Not showing it. 'You mustn't do that with Robin.'

'What?'

'I saw. Things aren't what they seem. You're next after me, with the gift.'

'You're talking nonsense.' Síon, in a vain attempt at nonchalance, smooths her already tame hair.

'The sight. The magic. It'll come on you when I'm dead and that'll be soon. But you got to have the truth.' She knows even when she says it that, like all of the young ones, Síon doesn't believe a thing about the old ways, so there's nothing for it but to prove it.

'Close your eyes.'

'Mamó?'

'Just close your eyes without the disagreement. I'm not your daft mother.' Síon does, and Sheldrú places her thumbs on her granddaughter's eyelids. 'Watch—'

Initially Síon sees nothing in the lush, pristine, primordial forest. Until she notices two naked bodies amongst the leaves and bracken.

Sheldrú is perhaps twenty. Pale and wild as one of the ponies out west on Ben Slievemore. She's making love with Robin who looks to be as he does now.

Many months later, two women sit up front of a vardo drawn by two horses, the one, a midwife also named Róisín but with the last name, Séala, the name of strangers from across the sea, from a clan not known to these people. She would later be taken in and her son Ailín, raised as their own.

Her story had been peculiar enough. She had been whisked away from a distant, little known island off the coast called Inishrún, hidden for most of the mist-shrouded year. She'd been taken to the mainland by the monks who'd said she was not right, that her mother had been a whore and that the father had been one of those visiting heathens. She was raised in an institution for wayward girls, her heritage seemingly forgotten.

She had escaped, stumbling across the gypsy encampment, half-starved. Unable, for the first few months, to say a word, her big dark eyes like those of a deer in headlights of a highway and unable to protect herself from catastrophe. Happening upon the only clan who would accept a child-woman, thought to maybe be a *changeling* for her gift of foretelling events long before they eventuated, but always able to alert them when the Garda were coming and so giving them time to pack up and move on. The tribe that was Billy Shando's. She'd explained she was Róisín Séala, but the church had forged papers and named her *Sheela Rose*.

At the time of Sheldrú's baby's birth the older Róisín was in her early thirties, a silent woman, thick with magic, who volunteered to make this journey and deliver this unwanted child, having also loved a man of the Fair Folk and carrying his son to birth.

Sheldrú, heavily pregnant, sits beside Róisín Séala as the vardo wends its way along the pitted track towards shelter, clutching at her massive belly, that cramps with early labor, to the pop and fart of the horses, the jangle of their brasses, the squeak of leather in the traces comforting and familiar.

Róisín Séala navigates the wagon, stopping at a pasture gate. She works the horses through the movement of her hands on the reins, controlling the traces and the swingletree with the skill of a lifetime on the road. Her long raven-black hair shot through with premature silver, is loose, as is fitting for a woman with the sight, owned by no marriage and moxado mostly, blowing about her face in the damp north wind.

Being alone without clan is a rare thing amongst gypsies but Sheldrú has broken the rules also, and got with child just like her companion, without naming the man who made her so, because he wasn't one and she couldn't say it without risking being hung as a witch.

No matter that she's been around other women giving birth, it still comes as a surprise when her waters break, the contractions merciless.

Róisín Séala, her own boy Ailín, then two, asleep in the furs at the rear of the wagon, knows where she is going. An ancient apple orchard beside a stream, the *patrin* on the gate-post a sign that her kind are welcome to stay a while.

Inside, beside the old combustion stove, Sheldrú howls with the pain of labor, waking a silent Ailín who sits chewing nervously on the corner of a cushion, only removing it long enough to eat his apple. After five hours of sweat and panting a head crowns.

Sheldrú bears down for the longest time, grunting and gritting her teeth, and eventually delivers a tiny infant, covered in the fine sheen of silver-blue caul that Róisín Séala carefully removes and places beside the hearth to preserve. Big magic, is the caul of a human infant. Can stop a masted ship from sinking, or so legends tell.

She ties the umbilicus and bites it in two with her teeth before she wraps the baby warmly, placing him in his mother's arms.

'Don't worry about a boy, Sheldrú, it's his own daughter who'll have the gifts. I know. Time for me to bear witness. What's his name to be then, so?' she says, stretching her back, her necklace of stones and talismans of bone, clinking with the bending, before she fills the kettle for tea, and refuels the stove.

'Gyofan.'

'And what will you give him as a family name?

'Borran. As good a name as any.'

'The others'll keep on for a while, just as they did for me. Cuppa tea?' When the younger woman nods, the midwife adds the condensed milk and makes sure the cup is cool enough so it doesn't burn the babe should Sheldrú spill a drop. 'I'll do what I can to hush the talk. You'll see, it'll be alright.'

Sheldrú attaches Gyofan to her breast, squalling with a voice that will define his entire life, as Ailín strokes the soft thick black hair of the newborn, a brother in all but blood.

And now, at castle Pook not far from where her father was conceived, Sheldrú removes her thumbs and Síon opens her eyes, confused and disturbed, shaking her head.

'Robin's your grandfather,' explains Sheldrú quietly enough. 'He doesn't age like mortals, so.

Síon is horrified. 'Mother Mary and all the saints. And I nearly—'

'You nearly did not.'

'And what do you mean, 'that'll be soon?'

'Don't mourn, *a cara*, I've been loved like most will never dream of, but I've seen it. My dead body under winter snow. And then the gift comes with the spring, and you can't not take it. I'm sorry if you wanted the choice because there isn't one.'

'Mamó, you know it doesn't snow in Ireland, hardly ever, so what're you on about? Ah, and about that, will it curse me to be unloved?'

Sheldrú is taken aback, shocked, folding Síon into her arms. 'Never.'

'So, Rose's father's daidí wasn't a man either?

Sheldrú shrugs, but there's that look in her eyes, 'There's some things it's ill-luck to talk about, so.'

'And you didn't answer my question.'

'Which one?'

The ancient roundhouse tower looms like a threat, within the rising mist of night's eventual darkness and the music is loud. The people chat in unrestrained joy, and laugh, cavort and sing, all around the central hearth. All those not involved in the ceremony to come, a little drunk or stoned. Gyofan dances alone.

Rose and Robin sit together, their heads close. When the music changes to a slow air Gyofan strides to her, wiping the sweat from his face with his neck bandana and waiting for them to permit him to speak.

'It's tomorrow night, then, for us to send off Ailín.' He's like a mountain, and even Robin is impressed at Gyofan's humility, aware that the gypsy has realized what their host really is, but undaunted, his attention on Rose and her needs. 'You alright with that?'

'Fine.'

He twists the bandana, retying it, damp, around his neck. 'Then you'll have your life back. Is that what we're to understand?'

'I'm sorry Gyofan. I know he was your friend. I just can't.'

'He was more than a friend, Róisín, and you're more than his daughter. You're also mine in all but blood. But I know. We're just glad you gave us the chance. The tradition and all. Their ghosts'll be together and they'll settle into the earth now. Please don't be bitter. You did the right thing.'

He walks away, grief-stricken. His eyes downcast, his chin trembling.

'Shit,' Rose sighs.

'What?' Robin moves as close as he dares. Rose takes an age to consider her response.

'Every time I think of my father I go cold inside. I think I hated him.'

'Why, Róisín?'

'He was broken.'

'How?'

'Why do you ask so many questions?'

'If you want I'll stop.

'No,' she says, pulling at her hair tie and tightening the plait even more.

'So why?' He wishes she'd just let the wind take the wild red she's so intent on imprisoning.

'He was always drunk. And he wouldn't shut up with the stories when I was around. Normal conversation was impossible and I could never talk about myself. I could never get a word in.'

'He loved you.'

'Then why wouldn't he even wash himself if I wasn't there to remind him? He'd even try telling me a story when he'd messed himself and I had him in the bath. If he was sober enough to even speak. Is neediness love, Robin?'

'*The jester walked in the garden: The garden had fallen still; He bade his soul rise upward and stand on her window-sill. It rose in a straight blue garment, when owls began to call: It had grown wise-tongued by thinking of a quiet and light footfall; but the young queen would not listen; She rose in her pale night-gown; she drew in the heavy casement and pushed the latches down.*'

'Yeats. From *The Cap and Bells*. Why that? What are you saying, Robin?'

'Maybe after he got lost the stories were all he had? A storyteller, a *seanchaí* we call them, can be like that. Cursed, some would say, and touched by the old gods, say others more knowing.'

Rose looks at him blankly, so he tries changing course. 'Come to the dance.'

'What? No. A funeral, Robin. I'm in mourning.'

'Please?'

He stands, brim-full of exuberance and Rose eventually shrugs, rising, hesitant.

The music changes to a lament and as the two touch body to body, Robin holds her firmly but sensuously.

Briefly a vision of wild revelry overshadows the campsite like a hallucination and she wonders, for a mere second, if some kind of mushroom might have been in the tea. Yet, with such a complex scene Rose stumbles. Robin, momentarily overjoyed, hurriedly adjusts his look to one of worry and helps her to sit.

'I *do* know you from somewhere. Or was I dreaming?'

'You've gone pale Róisín, I'll get some water,' he responds. 'Just sit. Wait for me.

...

12

THE BANGLE OF MANANNÁN MAC LÍR

SHELDRÚ, SÍON AND THE BROTHERS stand beside Gyofan, close enough to the blaze to be seen, but not so close as to burn like would have happened had the church caught them like this a hundred years ago.

Rose is intentionally alone holding the box.

'Twenty years gone,' says Gyofan, 'Orla Wen died in the town close to here. She became this place when her vardo burned. She's close, even tonight, because her ashes are bracken and the children of owls and foxes, mixed with soil and rain, under sun and moon as it is, but now I turn to Ailín's wish. He was lost to clan and culture from the moment his Orla died that way. Our man went into mourning, not ended, from what young Róisín here says, even as he's died.

'So now his girl has come all these miles to bring his ghost home proper like, and I'll pass you on to her now. Róisín?'

Rose is unmoving. Void. The slight smell of polish lifted by the fire's intensity from the box reminding her of the garden shed out back of 64 Lafayette Street when her dad was busy in solitude. She hadn't known he was making this. A deep wolf-in-a-trap howl is somewhere between her gut and her throat and she is trying to make sense of this feeling. Once the trap is opened, however, there'll be no knowing if the wolf will follow instinct and attack. The thought of feeling anything terrifies her.

His shade is close, and many others of mist, moonlight and shadow but so is her mother. She gathers her wits, blocks out the whispers of the long-dead and focuses on the moment knowing she has to say something, anything, to have this finished. To seal the lock.

'I'm sorry Dad,' she admits. 'What happened to you was a terrible way to die and there's a good cop hunting down your killers but you were a real bastard, you know that? And now I find out you were some kind of gypsy king and that's supposed to mean something when it can't. Because you never told me the truth. You talked but you never let me in. Is this enough now? Have I done enough this time?'

Confused faces don't understand what she's been through. They know shame, sure, but they know it together and they have pride because they also have always had each other and their secrets and a way of understanding. Rose hasn't. She's just never been like the people around her and what? Do they smell difference? An animal from an unacceptable pack? Even Gyofan and Sheldrú don't know, even though they think they do, what she's gone through with him. Only Robin, an immortal in a mortal world overrun by people who deny his existence except as a kind of once-upon-a-time-ness idea, knows.

Rose clears her throat, glances at Robin then back to the box. She gives Ailín the *Wandering Angus*, the story he loved most.

'*Though I am old with wandering through hollow lands and hilly lands, I will find out where she has gone, and kiss her lips and take her hands; and walk among long dappled grass, and pluck till time and times are done, the silver apples of the moon, the golden apples of the sun.* Fare well, Dáidí.'

Robin joins her in her isolation, taking one of her hands that she immediately pulls back. She's ready to return to the camp but it seems her people are not.

Billy Shando comes to the fire and lifts the horsehair, plaited in red thread, from the box.

'Me it was that married Ailín's mother who was also called Róisín,' he says to Rose. 'Did you know that Rose? Did he tell you?'

She shakes her head because he'd never talked of family, or these people. Only Orla. Only the killing. Her grandmother had died at her birth, her legacy, Rose's secret bag of her treasured things, that has always exuded power—hers alone—is back at the Lafayette Street house.

'Your grandmother was a deliverer of babies and a teller of fortunes, from all any of us know of her. It's told that she'd been banished for getting a child inside herself without saying from who. A terrible thing to keep secret from your people, you understand?

'One day she wandered into our camp with your daddy, a lad of perhaps seven. I took one look and loved her from the start. She was as fair as an apple tree in spring to my eyes with a wide-open honesty about her. A silence filled with secrets. A knowing, so? She never wanted to talk about who or what planted Ailín in her except that he came from some island off this wild west coast. Some say she was loved by a man of the Fair Folk but it didn't matter to me. I took your *daidí* and raised him. My son in all but blood.'

Billy Shando walks around the fire and lifts the tassel high for all to see.

'One year we was at Ballinasloe, for the horse fair. Ailín was fourteen at the time. He sees this pied stallion, with a snow white tail and a snow-white mane and he has to have him.

'A nasty brawl breaks out with another man who's chasing after the same beast and it's our lad's first fight. I'm shit-scared he'll have his arse kicked but he doesn't. He wants that horse so bad he gets him.

'He called him Manannán mac Lír and he had him till Orla died, when he set him to roam with the wild horses and sire a thousand foals, where I think he is to this day. So this is his talisman. Bound horse and man as one. Hair from the tail of that magpie stallion and the red thread of Orla's funeral measure, the other. Stories she never shared with me.

'Manannán mac Lír was his brother in all but blood and I consign the bond to the fire as is right, so their ghosts are released from any curse, to fly over the ocean to Tír na n'Óg.'

He throws the horse hair tied with ribbon into the flames and takes out the animal pelt and unrolls it, the fur like sunset in the glow of the bonfire.

'It's from a fox, I think. Róisín Séala used to wear it, said it was her *luck*. I passed it on to Ailín when she died because she'd warned it wasn't destiny that it burns with herself and the rest of her things. Not one of her other charms or talismans were to be found ever after, just so you know. A mystery to this very day.'

Rose drops her gaze so none can see her lies; hiding her knowledge of where they are.

'But I guess it's just a story now.' He toes the ground. 'So be done with it all, it is.'

He throws the hide into the fire and the color of the flames changes to an eerie green and blue. The gypsies are silent with superstitious fear.

'I don't know, he continues, 'about the rest of the stuff.'

'I do,' says Sheldrú. She has the glitter-red shoe in one hand, and the bound and woven mane of horse and human hair in the other, a bangle of brightly colored thread woven through with beads of amber and blue glass, tiny bones and thin tubes of gold. She has rolled it in spruce and oak resin, as her own mother once taught her so it is more like something worn by a woman of the Fair Folk and hidden away, because. A twining of many lives.

She shows the shoe to everyone, being very certain Rose is paying attention, while the ornate bangle is crooked by her index finger.

'This was your first walking shoe Róisín. He kept it because he laid a geis upon it. He said, *as long as I live I'll keep this shoe. My wish upon it is that wherever she walks, she does so to her own story and no one else's.*'

'Is that the truth or are you just trying to pull me in?' Rose is stricken. Confused by these strangers who seem to know her life better than she does. Also angry in a way she's used to, that has never made sense.

Sheldrú doesn't hesitate when she tosses it onto the fire but she holds the bangle high. 'The hair is his and Orla's. And that of Manannán mac Lír. And yours, from when it first grew long and looked like light reflecting off a new penny. This shouldn't go on the fire, Róisín. You need to keep it so your own love and your own children get woven in with their own lives.'

Rose steels herself to say what finally she must. 'I don't know you people, and I won't be having children, and besides, this—' she takes the charm from Sheldrú, claiming it as her own for just a moment before assigning it to the heart of the blaze. 'Doesn't matter. I don't really know any of you or anything of what this is all about. I don't remember and I've never lived as one of you. It is not my intention to offend anyone, you've all been wonderful, but I'd be pretending, and I'm done with secrets and fanciful half-truths about animal people and Fair Folk, and *Róisín, did I tell you the one about.* All of it.'

She burns the letter, upends the box. The photographs, the book of Yeats' poetry. It takes the flame. Lastly she throws on the box. It takes the blaze in disturbing blues and greens. She turns and stumbles the way they'd all come, along the now bent and broken bracken track.

She's on her rock a short time later. She pours a thimble of whisky, from the flask Síon gave her just in case, into a tin cup and downs it in one gulp before wrapping her quilted jacket more tightly around herself, the night so very cold away from the bonfire with only a small hearth kept burning near the Bedford.

Robin, alone, hands dug deep in his pockets, his face a frown that studies the ground, joins her. He says nothing.

'Are we the only normal people here?' she asks, after a while.

'Define normal?' His mouth twitches as he tries not to smile.

He scuffs at stones with a booted foot, no other expression giving cause for suspicion. Yet one by one and two by two, as the gypsies return, they glance in his direction as though they had heard.

Rose is the only person oblivious to what Robin is, it seems.

'I should never have come and now I've offended them, and they've been really nice to me.'

'Well it seems to me you have done what was you believed was necessary.' He pats her hand but she pulls it away again thinking the gesture patronizing.

'Did.'

'What?'

'Sorry.'

'So?'

'So, Robin, where's the nearest hotel because I really need a hot shower and a private room. To be away from this.'

'My house has got two bedrooms. I can offer you lodging for as long as you need. Freely given. No strings. I promise.'

Rose thinks a world of memories and possibilities are released like a frozen waterfall. She is filled with trepidation and resolve in equal measure. 'You're not an axe murderer or anything are you?' she asks, thinking she's being humorous. He gives her his Jack Nicholson *Shining* grin. Yet, as Rose makes up her mind he keeps hidden the fact he considers this hilarious.

'I'll get some of my stuff.'

She emerges from the Bedford juggling her backpack, hand luggage and laptop, squeezing her notebook down the front of the zippered section of her computer case.

'Did you come with just this?'

She hands him the backpack without biting. 'I'll meet you at the bike, smarty pants.'

She confronts Gyofan who tolerates Sheldrú working the knots and tangles from his hair with a curry comb. Rose rummages in her handbag, brings out a piece of paper and a pen and writes. 'This is my address. Can you please send anything I've forgotten there? I'm really sorry to have to ask.'

Gyofan pulls away from his mother. 'Róisín, what're you doing?'

'She's going with Robin,' Sheldrú states.

'He's offered. Can I trust him?' asks Rose

'I do.' Sheldrú remains stoic even though her heart is breaking.

There's a silence within the already still night. Then the wind comes up, the clouds moving like giant ships across the waning moon, promising rain before dawn. Sheldrú whispers, '*Go raibh míle maith agat,* Róisín. A blessing, hoping that life is kind.'

Rose repeats the expression until she says it correctly this once, knowing she's unlikely to hear either Irish or Shelta again after she returns to her real life. She hitches her leg over the pillion of the bike, and Robin navigates the pitted, rutted road, not caring to slow down at all.

The north wind now has intent as its breath, and Sheldrú hears her name on it. Robin's voice. *I'll love you always, my lovely cailín, whether earth or fate, or even all the stars in the sky.*

'As will I, you,' she whispers.

'What?' Gyofan will probably never truly know his mother.

13

IF WISHES WERE HORSES

A STORM WOULD HAVE PASSED IN THE night because in its wake is a brilliantly vitalized sunny day that only comes of such. Robin's house is a traditional whitewashed stone cottage with a thatched roof, near a sheer drop to the rocks below. A pick-up truck is in a carport alongside Robin's motorbike. The ocean is loud as it seeks the highest ledges of land, as are the sea birds that nest in niches of the cliff, safe from predation.

Rose wakes in a quaint room, stretches, considers life and its spurious grasp on meaning and purpose, then eventually dresses. She navigates her way to the kitchen and to a pair of French doors open onto a terraced garden.

'Morning,' Robin chimes, happily cooking a fry-up breakfast.

'I smell coffee and bacon,' she muses.

'Here or out there?'

'Outside's good. Can I help?'

The hot fat spits at him and his eyes darken for a moment, as though the pan was a dragon full of spite, before his smile lights up for her. 'Grab us those cups. Knives and forks are in that drawer. Or we could eat with our fingers.'

The little courtyard is paved with slate. High stone walls line either side, blocking off the wildest of the sea wind that can come like a gale and that does so in winter and spring, as it has done for a thousand, thousand years.

It stops right at the edge of the cliff and has a clear view out over the ocean, whitecaps like the manes of horses.

Small beds of forget-me-nots, violets, dandelion and terracotta pots of red geraniums add to the sense of a home well-tended. Gulls and gannets fill the air with their important conversations.

Rose shields her eyes from the sky's dazzle and looks to the horizon. She sits at a wrought iron table and chairs. Robin joins her with breakfast.

'Feeling better?' he asks, handing her a plate of toast, fried eggs, bacon, blood sausage and other unrecognizable possibilities she has no intention of eating.

'Like I just woke up from some really weird dream.'

'There's a beautiful cove at the bottom of a little path. We can even swim if you're keen.'

'Not appropriate.'

'Wear undies if you're shy.' He's reading her mind, but she doesn't figure that out. 'But I don't wear clothes in the sea. It's about as intelligent as dressing for a bath.' He tucks into the food like a man starving.

Late morning. They carry towels over their shoulders as they navigate the suicidal track down the side of the cliff. Rose is fully dressed, even though Robin is only in jeans, his feet bare. She can't help but glance sidelong at his tattoo-storied body, confused at her admiration.

He holds her hand for much of the way, like she's feeble or ancient. She lets him because she's a city woman and yes, she's scared of falling. They reach the small, sheltered beach surrounded by high cliffs, where seals bob up and down, now their heads watching, now dropping below the water, unconcerned. Their interest inscrutable.

Robin strips completely and bounds into the slate grey and indigo sea like a puppy while Rose watches on feeling like a voyeur. For a short time. Eventually, she removes her clothes and joins him for all of two icy minutes.

Cold and shivering, chicken-skinned and slightly blue, she runs to the towels and holds one around herself like a shawl. The day may be hot but the water off the west coast is off the arctic and her teeth knock uncontrollably, exultant.

Robin stays hip deep in the sea, his back to her. Two seals pass around him and he touches one with delicate fingers as it slides beneath his hand. He swims with them, racing them. It's useless, pointless, and she can hear him laughing and calling to them in Irish. Then the seals are gone. He turns towards land, ploughs through the waves and races up the beach, grabbing the other towel.

'You're peculiar, you know that?'

Robin is breathless. She's hard work. He knew she would be, just not to this extent.

'*Somewhere,*' he takes a great shuddering breath, '*ages and ages hence: two roads diverged in a wood, and I—I took the one less traveled by, and that has made all the difference.*'

'Frost isn't it? What road is the one that you're traveling?'

Robin ponders, but not for long. He's always known the why of her question. It's what sets him apart from the other púca. 'I had a choice about that once upon a time. Once upon a time I could have had just about anything I wanted.'

'Your family rich or something?'

'Beyond your wildest dreams Róisín. But I chose love.'

'Couldn't you have both? That hardly seems fair.'

'Fair is it?' He laughs and waits, but she doesn't have a comeback, either that or she's listening for once. 'Not according to them. If I'd done life their way it would have been work, work, work and people would have meant nothing.'

'That's sad. Do you love them just a little?'

Robin is dumbstruck that she can't hear herself asking him almost the same questions he asked her about her father, but he knows not to ruin the moment. 'Oh yes. And they're fair about my choice. Doesn't stop them loving me. It's just different, how I choose to be alive.'

'But you still own a lot of property.'

'Róisín. I *am* it.'

'That's a very environmentalist way of saying the same thing, isn't it?'

'Not the way I see it. Do you know this? '*I could not but choose the hardest way. To follow the seasons and support the majesty of the years. To sow the seed and to watch it thrust through the soil; to call the flower from its hiding place and give it strength to nestle its own life.'*

'I don't know that.'

'Kahlil Gibran. So I chose love.'

'And what do you love, Robin?'

He gestures widely, wildly, the enormity of her question washing through him. 'All this. Everything I can. Us.'

'Us?'

'You want to go up and get some lunch?'

'I can't tell when you're serious or when you're playing the jester.'

Robin grins, stands and pulls on his jeans. He holds out his hand and helps Rose to her feet. 'Race you to the top.'

Rose, sand in her mouth along with rebellious strands of her copper hair, wipes at her tongue, distracted. 'Not going to happen, urchin.'

He bounds off, heedless as to whether she is following. Knowing she will. Rose dresses slowly, trying to calm her rattled mind.

She climbs up the sand to where Robin sits at the entrance to the track up the cliff side. 'I thought you might need a hand up.'

'I'm not that old.'

He can't help himself. He laughs aloud.

Gyofan has hold of the wheel in an iron grip, steering the Bedford with all his strength, concentrating on the road. Crammed together on the bench seat beside him are Sheldrú and Síon, with Billy Shando and the lads all bunched up together in back. The windows are down and there are big cars, caravans and trailers behind and in front. A convoy headed in the same direction, north along the coast. A sad day indeed.

'What will happen to her?' Gyf asks of no one in particular.

'She'll fall in love with him of course,' says Sheldrú, knowing. 'And he'll stay with her as long as he can.'

'Think she'll ever come back to us?' He has trouble clutching into fifth gear, bemoaning the warning of the grind.

'Who knows?'

'You've seen, old woman, you're being obscure, so,' says Gyofan, hardly knowing his mother at all.

'Just watch the fecken road or you'll kill us,' she adds, 'I don't believe we're going back to that shithole after this.'

'I wouldn't mind a visit with her when it works out to be right,' Síon murmurs, her mind already made up, what with Rose being her sister in all but blood.

'That's a grand plan,' Sheldrú says intuitively. 'She'll need one of us sometime soon.'

Billy Shando reaches across the back of the driver's seat to be heard by Gyofan. 'Can you let me out on your way back? Before the inland road.'

'Not coming for the craic at the tower?'

'No' admits Billy, contrite. 'I made a promise to God about a few things. I got a debt to pay, now.'

Gyofan grunts and turns on the radio that plays an old Janis Joplin song.

Rose showers behind the bath curtain when Robin barges in. Her first reaction, despite earlier, is embarrassment. He sits on the closed toilet seat, excited and pleased with himself. 'Want to go clubbing tonight?'

She pokes her head around the curtain. 'Where?'

'You *know* I know places, Róisín. Bit of a craic after all the deadly seriousness.'

'Can you please go away while I get dressed?'

'But, I seen you in the sea.'

'Robin.'

He gets up, head hanging.

'And yes, I'd love to.'

He closes the door soundlessly.

That evening in the never-ending summer twilight the motorcycle purrs along the back roads all the way into the city of Cork itself, where they park out front of the pub called the *Ceili*, an impossibility if it wasn't a Monday. They dance to a local band and drink Guinness and laugh. And flirt.

Later in the night, with the sweat drying on their bodies and the yellow streetlights casting their skins eerie, they promenade the pavements, wander the grounds of Fitzgerald Park, eat hot chips from paper bags. They stop by the buskers and performers still high on methamphetamines and likely in the same locale when trade picks up again come Thursday. Robin pays them ample coin. His destiny not twined with theirs, therefore not caring what becomes of them when he's not there to appreciate the music.

One last stop happens at Coughlan's Bar. For a shot of their famous gin. Robin then fills the bike with gas and rides them home, following the coast, a little like traveling with death.

In her pajamas Rose makes tea for them both. Robin lights the peat fire before putting a vinyl on the record player and carefully lowering the diamond stylus. Traditional Irish folk music that she seems to love like only a visitor could.

Despite the chill they take the tea outside and sit on the grass near the cliff-edge. He kisses her. She does not stop him.

He rolls her onto her side and slides his hand under her shirt touching the skin he's waited so long to know. First off she flinches like he's burned her, then there's nothing she won't do as he carries her into the cottage, and trips, unromantically but painlessly, propelling them both onto the pile of fluffy rugs before the fire. The intensity broken by his trickster antics.

She learns just how fine a man's hands are when all she's ever done is read about it. Never even being courageous enough to watch an erotic video, let alone porn.

They make love on the carpet in the warmth of the smoldering peat, the dull, eerie light of the last of the waning moon sending the spirits of the land into the corners of the room, reducing reality to shadow and memory.

Rose wakes in a tangle of sheets. At some stage they must have ended up in here although it's all a blur after the first time she pulled him inside her, so she has no way of knowing whose idea a soft bed with clean white sheets must have been.

Robin is flat on his back, fast asleep, one arm across her body, making small snoring sounds.

She slides out from under him and turns on her side to watch his breath, his lips, his dark shaggy, curly hair, the rise and fall of him. Her face is shadow and sun, lightning storm and desert. Her eyes read every contour of him as his eyes move beneath closed lids, him dreaming, his expression changing moment to moment, his mouth murmuring nonsense. Grinning in sleep.

She doesn't so much whisper, as mouths, 'You are so splendid, you strange man. And I'm sorry, so sorry, I really am,' and she pads to take a shower, her shoulders resigned.

The bathroom is full of steam when she hears the toilet seat lift. Hears him peeing. 'So what do you want to do today?'

She turns off the taps and drapes herself in the silly beachball-patterned towel, not the slightest bit shy anymore but still finding his candidness uncomfortable. 'Stop doing that.'

She's dressed when she comes to the small bright kitchen, but Robin isn't. He's scrambling eggs. 'You're not self-conscious at all, are you?' she says, chin in her hands at the bench.

'You want what I'm having? I cracked enough.'

'I bet you did. You got any fruit?

He stops whisking and goes pale, a moment of sheer immortal, faerie panic. 'Oh. Fruit! I can do fruit.'

He opens the fridge and summons up a spell that would put a younger faerie out for a week. He brings out blueberries and mangos and papaya and passion fruit, apples and lychees and red currents. He places them on the table, as naturally as breathing.

Rose piles it all into a big bowl and carries it into the garden while he makes them thick sweet Turkish coffee.

They idle away the morning, feeding each other, laughing and summoning poetry about silly things. As often as they can, touching and experiencing each other. She says nothing, yet, of what she has decided.

Towards midday Robin goes into the house, coming back later in jeans, walking carefully with brim-full mugs of hot chocolate.

Rose blacks out her cell phone screen as he sits beside her, worried, handing her a mug. 'Where's the craic, so?'

'I've booked my flights,' she mumbles under her breath, so softly even he, with the hearing of a wolf, can barely make out the reality. At first not believing it. It takes him many breaths to gather his raveled feelings into a gentle question.

'Why Róisín?' This was not the plan.

Rose is uncomfortable and a little ashamed at her lie, but is determined not to show it. 'I need to get back.'

'You're afraid.' He's not asking. He knows.

'Of what?'

'Of love.'

'Rubbish.'

He's so close to her she can feel his breath on her lips. 'What if I say I love you, Rose?'

'I'd say we only just met and that you're deluded.' *My god*, she thinks, realizing this for what? The first time? *Rose Wen, you're such a fraud.*

'What about last night?'

She tosses her messed up, tangled hair, turns away and pretends at flippancy, the lie coming harder than ever this time. 'Last night was great but now I've got to go home and finish what I started.'

'I love you.'

'My flight's at six tomorrow morning,' she says, making light. 'Nuts huh? I probably should stay in Dublin this evening as I have to check in ages beforehand. How do I get to the airport from here? Is there a bus?'

'Shut up, please Róisín.'

'I have to go.'

'I'll drive you, but stop.'

'What?'

He kisses her. She tries to pull away. He coaxes her back, kisses her again. She lets it happen. Returns the passion doubly. She could so easily get lost here. Again. And never get back. Never leave. Knowing that love doesn't last.

He has his arms around her, so very serious. 'Say it, Rose.'

'No.'

'Say, I love you Robin Kipling.'

'No.'

He waits. She doesn't change her mind. 'So soon it'll be too late.'

'I'm sorry.'

'If I had a penny for every time you said that.' He changes from the threat of snow to sun on a pristine lake. In seconds. He has to. She'll bolt like a wild pony if he doesn't rein himself in, and he knows it. 'Let's have a swim and then go to the cafe and spend some money on books. All that stuff. Will you just hang out with me? I'll drive you in the dark before dawn.'

She's hesitant, and somehow afraid, but it's not logical, so she thinks it's just her fear of herself losing control. 'Yes. Okay.'

The light is so silver that it's impossible to know where the ocean ends, and the sky begins as the front door is pulled closed behind them.

Robin is dressed in his cleanest denims, T shirt, old earthen colored waistcoat with leather buttons and an antique silver fob chain leading to somewhere in a pocket and wearing his well-loved, frayed silk top hat. He eventually starts the reluctant pick-up and the truck coughs awake. Rose takes one last look at the cottage.

That old rust bucket bumps down the track towards the highway, and Robin and Rose's eyes are fixed on the road ahead, him seeming to look for potholes that could crack the axle while actually keeping the spell strong so she never thinks to turn the way they've come.

If she'd even looked in the rear view mirror once, or turned, out of nostalgia, to fix the image of them together in her memory, had seen through the back window, she'd be met with a stunning but barren coast, seals way out in the pewter water, bull kelp lashing the shore from some wild, unseen storm that shook the world, way off in the North Sea at some time during the night. Rainbow, through the mist, hitting landfall.

Wild, clean and beautiful, but no house.

...

14

A COAT OF MANY POEMS

AT THE AIRPORT ROSE CHECKS HER BAGGAGE and the SMS with her boarding details. She scans the departure and arrival screen before joining Robin who's sulking in the airport cafe.

'Flight's on time.'

Robin had removed his hat and his hair is going every which way, messy and ragged as a crow in the wind, momentarily looking up at her from his coffee before returning his gaze to the dregs as though to an oracle that could, today and finally, predict his impossible death.

'Don't you dare make me feel guilty,' she pouts. Grumpy with lack of sleep and sad, because she doesn't know what else to do but what she's doing.

'Will you change your mind?'

She touches his soft mouth with a finger, as though to say don't speak. No argument. She's only just sat down with her order when the Dublin to London flight, FR112, calls the passengers to the gate. Robin and Rose look at each other in unspoken disbelief. Here it is, then.

He wanders with her to the security checkpoint.

Rose stows her laptop and handbag, boots and belt in the grey plastic trays while Robin, one hand in his jeans pockets, the other holding his hat like a supplicant, watches her, seeming resigned.

She throws her arms around his neck and kisses him with everything in her and he holds her, a groan escaping his lips that nuzzle her neck in hope. But no, she pulls away and squats down, the silliest thing she can think of, studying the hole in her sock where her big toe pokes through. She pulls the fabric closed, knowing full well the futility. 'It always happens to just the one,' she says, as though it matters.

'It's like the curse of Cú Chulainn.' Robin's eyes are alight with the memory of the warrior-turned-hound for a year.

She smiles that funny look of confusion she gets when she's out of her depths and he laughs, both of them forcing lightheartedness.

'No time.' She doesn't dare breathe as the enormity of her decision to abandon him hits her.

'No time. Never time. This it then, so?' he says, defeated.

'I'm sorry.'

She tears up and her chin has a mind of its own. He squats beside her, and they duck-waddle out of the way of the passengers banked up behind her, waiting to pass through the scanner.

'Wen?'

She takes a moment to even react to him, let alone say it. 'I really do love you.'

Robin's face is the summer, and the night before, and his kisses and all the poetry he's ever said.

'Ah, Sweet Mother Mercy,' he groans in protest to the air around them. Then, 'I'll find you, Róisín. I'll come. Is that okay?'

'Promise?'

People in the queue smile, as people do at lovers. Relating to the desperation of goodbyes.

'I promise.'

Rose kisses his nose. She stands, adjusts her clothing and moves away through the metal detector, her toe escaping its confines again in defiance at her earlier stupid act. At her pretense.

'Bejesus, wait up!' He radiates astonishment at how something this important could almost have slipped his mind. He pulls the bangle of tightly plaited hair, with wires of gold and silver, of uncountable bright colors, with beads of amber and blue glass, laced with tiny bones and thread-thin tubes of gold and rolled in spruce and oak resin, so it is more like something worn, once, by the queen of some storybook faerie, and hidden away forever, than of the twining of people's lives. 'Róisín, you forgot your matháir's *ting.*'

Her jaw drops and her heart races. She worries, unnecessarily, about what the detectors or security might do. She summons all her courage to smile and say sorry, as she takes it from his hand, explaining it to the security woman. 'It's a family keepsake. He was caring for it while I took a swim,' before slipping it onto her wrist, the magic so strong that no guard or inspector wonders at all the animal parts.

She locks eyes with Robin for a final time, his enchantment at not allowing her to see behind her intentionally lifted, her not needing to question how what was burned in that fire could now be whole. Finally comprehending that he is not quite a mortal man. The myriad of events of confusion clearing as though a fog of perpetual obscurity has finally revealed the summit of an until-now unrealized height.

The pale summer day calls the cloud to the sky outside the wide windows of the terminal as Robin, a púka from outside of time, watches the plane taxi along the runway, take off and begin the ascent. He turns without looking back, a knowing smile lighting his animal eyes. He replaces his hat and whistles low, to himself, as he strolls towards the exit.

Inside the airplane most of the interior lights are switched off and many of the passengers are asleep as an unseasonable thunderstorm lashes the channel, shaking the plane and reminding everyone of the frailty of life.

Rose has her eyes closed, twisting the bangle idly and intentionally if such a thing can be. She's in an aisle seat beside a young woman of Vietnamese heritage, with a shaved head and big hoop earrings through stretched earlobes, evocative tattoos under each ear, baggy overalls and a loose red silk shirt.

She takes Rose's left hand, thinking her companion afraid. Rose continues writing in her art journal with her other hand: *I have touched you with the poems of many ages. I have wrapped around you colors from a forest deep and ancient, I have loved your body clean of rage, enough I hope, for you to know it for the disillusionment of those who'd hunt you down, the spirit of you, wild; enchanted, lost on concrete streets that know no giving. And I know how long it's haunted you through all the times you challenged trust to find it only endless dust.*

Rose lets her pen go still, weeping soundlessly, a tissue to her nose to catch the leaking, taking back her hand from the other woman and booting up her laptop before typing. *I see you in the forest deep, wild rose and mosses at your feet and mists, like ghosts, between huge trees; I see you gently bend your knees and kiss the earth with lips and tears,*

'Is London home?' asks the stranger beside her.

'No. And I've got seventeen hours before my connecting flight,' Rose smiles, powering down her laptop and securing it in the computer case.

'And it's a Saturday. So this is destiny. I'm Molly by the way.'

The seat-belt lights come on as Rose gives her name and the two swap small talk.

A man's deep, lighthearted voice over the intercom says, 'Cabin crew prepare for landing.'

'Do you want to share a taxi with me to Camden Town? The best market in London. Magic, I promise.' She buckles up and stows away her tray table.

'Magic *and* promises, Molly?'

'Ha. I won't be able to show you around though. I'm on a food rescue run for the C4WS.'

'Oh?'

'Homelessness is out of control since the collapse. C4WS is a project for them.'

'Yes, I'll do the market.'

...

After wandering the unfamiliarity and fascination of Camden Market Rose is done in, ready to leave. It hasn't taken her long. It never does. She's not a shopper.

She has plenty of time, so she strolls down the very end isle, right up next to the old Pickford Stables.

And straight into a retro stall with everything from jet, jade and rhinestone jewelry to Carnaby Street fashion. Sequined masks. Old gramophones and the furs of long dead, sad animals. There is something about the smell of the booth that she doesn't quite place. Is it the violet-scented face powder from the nineteen twenties? The balls of old wool shorn from Argyle sheep? Something familiar that she can't name, but utterly irresistible for all that? A forest where no tree has been cut down? Absinth in Paris or the sawdust on the ground of the big top in a carnival? A peat fire or a roundhouse castle that once beheld wonder? Hot chips in newspaper? Whatever, it draws her to the exotic and odd.

She sees the coat. The last thing in her life, before today, she would ever have bought. High, stiff rabbit fur collar, an outer layer of dark, chocolate-colored velvet embroidered with secrets, lined with pink slipper satin, and long enough to sweep the floor like some medieval bridal gown. Something silly but crafted perfectly. Renaissance. A patchwork of colors and fabrics stitched together flawlessly, a hand embroidered peacock down the back and peace signs at each cuff. Beaded here and there with pearls and tiny limpet shells.

A piece of her father. The gypsies. Robin.

A memory, like the bangle on her wrist.

The A330 flies out of London in the evening to arrive at the airport nine miles south of New Rathmore on the morning of the same day she'd left Dublin. A twist in time not missed by Rose who has continued with her poem for most of the journey.

…The memory of such a man who loves with love like none before; who met me—left me wanting more—at ocean's edge at summer's height, will give the gods, the woman who is gypsy-born, the ravens and the rose's thorns, good reasons for continued dawns.

'That's stunning.'

She closes the art book and clutches it to her chest, giving the stranger the kind of look that would slice paper.

'I loved a man like that once,' he confides.

He's Jeremy Farrell and he's irresistibly debonair and fun. They exchange a little of each other's histories. Rose tells of Oscar Wilde, who was sent to prison for being homosexual, and of robbers who broke into his house while he was away for the day. 'The story goes that he came home in the middle of the theft, and when they threatened to cause him grievous bodily harm he suggested they take anything they needed, but that they join him for lunch first.'

Jeremy is in stitches over that, but then she recites the whole of the *Ballad of Reading Gaol*, about that little patch of blue and each man killing the things he loves, and he veers the other way and cries and cries, utterly unembarrassed. Rose talks about herself and college and English and teaching, and he explains that he learned his trade as a hacker when he was twelve years old. The Dark Net. And then had to work his way up to becoming legit. That now he does IT for festivals.

He's just returning from Glastonbury with a phone full of new contacts, and the memory of lots of really good drugs.

He keeps her laughing with his no-nonsense approach to money and politics, sex and religion for most of the long haul. They share the screen for *How To Train Your Dragon IV*, cheering at the same time, holding their breath at the same time and shedding tears of joy over the ending at the same time, until, at last, the man on the intercom with the same deep voice says, 'Ladies and Gentlemen we are beginning our descent into the beautiful city of New Rathmore. The weather down on the ground is—'

Rose unashamedly reaches across Jeremy to peer out the window at the pristine wilderness of the ranges, snow-capped all year round, in the distance and Mount Revenant, the caldera of a once-volcanic mountain in the heart of what had been a trading city that prospered on death. Him using her head as a pillow in order to also see, whilst simultaneously stroking the collar of her coat and purring.

'—a beautiful twenty-three degrees and the sun is shining beneath cotton candy cloud. On behalf of myself and the cabin crew we'd like to thank you for flying with the A330. If you're coming home welcome back, otherwise enjoy your time here.'

While they wait at the carousel for their luggage Rose tells Jeremy about her father's death and of staying with the gypsies. That she is one and had lived her whole life never knowing. But she says nothing of Robin.

'A bit like me and my grandparents,' he chuckles.

'They don't know you're gay?'

'They're dead, love.'

'It's a good thing you don't believe in an afterlife then, isn't it?'

He laughs with his head thrown back, before his luggage leaves the little rubber opening, then he hugs her, his eyes teary again.

When he pulls the suitcases off the turnstile he holds out his hand to her, tipping his head and pursing his lips.

'What?' she asks.

'Phone, Wen.'

She gives him her cell phone and he adds his details to her contacts, showing her the entry.

'We clear? I want action, Wendy. I want more Wilde stories, I want to be there for the release of the book of these poems you are writing, and when you are dead I want your coat.'

Summer passes and Rose reclaims the life she thought she'd wanted. Studying and repeating the rituals, the unthinking, rote habits developed over a lifetime. So easy to fall into when she is alone. No challenges or surprises. No one to care for.

She has coffee and movie dates with Jeremy for the relief of his company, and he teaches her to pirate.

Her one-bedroom apartment, on the third floor of the now weathered, once beautiful private mansion that had been built on the fur trade, is her sanctuary. Or so she tells herself. And she almost—almost—never thinks about what happened with the death of her father. That it was all merely a dream, the notebooks filled with her journaling of what happened, and the poetry, long since abandoned in the bottom of her kitchen drawer.

This year is one of the coldest winters on record, with snowfall and black ice causing chaos; the closures of schools and amenities over much of the city, once, earlier in the month, for several days. Only the airports, the rail and city bus services are still functioning, almost as usual and the brave, maybe stupid, taxi drivers of New Rathmore Metropolitan.

Rose, in for the night, types up her lecture notes when a soft knock breaks the silence. The laptop screen reads 21:54.

'Who is it?' she calls, wary, the big freeze summoning the desperate and mean to invade people's homes with them there.

'Róisín,' shivers a familiar voice. 'It's Síon. And I'm frozen.'

Rose pushes back her chair and yanks the door open. Síon is rugged up against the cold, has a battered suitcase in her hand and, although grinning, is shaking uncontrollably.

'Fecken deadly out there,' she says, the thin wool coat no protection against the arctic blast. 'It's colder in this country than at Santa's house, Róisín.'

Rose grabs her. Hugs her almost to the point of cracking ribs. She then takes her suitcase and pulls her inside.

'Why didn't you let me know, I'd have met you. What have you got in here, a body?'

'Shut up, yourself,' Síon laughs, removing gloves, an oversized puffer jacket, pink high profile baseball cap, and looking for a mirror.

'Here, give me those.' Rose opens the bedroom door and places Síon's outer layers on the bed, while Síon hefts the case up as well.

'Is this where you sleep, Róisín?' she says, grinning with mirth. 'You know I hate sharing, unless you're a film star with a huge cock, which you're not.'

Rose is laughing at the unchanged attitude, but is surprised at the certain something her sister-in-all-but-blood exudes. A self-confidence and mystery. Like a translucent film of nacre.

'It's fine. Look at you!' Rose hugs Síon again before pulling her by the hand into the sitting room. 'You want tea? Coffee? Are you hungry?'

Síon sits on the edge of the settee, admiring the relative affluence. 'Sheldrú died. And so's Billy Shando.'

Matter of fact. Rose's inner world is shattered, memories of alive people now broken mirror pieces that she can't pretend don't matter. 'How?'

'She went in her sleep two weeks ago. Smile on her face.' Rose sits beside her, stunned. 'We'd talked not long before. She asked me to come. Can I have that tea?'

'What's wrong with me. Please, make yourself at home. It's as much your place as mine.' Rose switches on the electric kettle, gets cups and things, clumsy and distracted. 'And Billy?'

'Strangest thing,' Síon reflects, 'He'd come back to us after years and years. You know he lived here to keep an eye on your father, don't you? Did you know he was once a priest?'

'I knew none of it, Síon.'

'Well, he wasn't the same man, says Gyofan, when he comes home. Scared. Really scared. Daidí saw it, so did Sheldrú. Something had happened, and he never said what. Died in a chapel, he did. Heart, the doctor wrote it up as. Fright, said Sheldrú, herself dead not a week later.' Síon examines the palms of her hands, looking for signs of destiny. 'Róisín,' she adds softly, apologetically, 'I got my own money.'

'Síon. We're sisters, aren't we? I'm so glad you're here.'

'In all but blood, so it is, *a cara*.' Síon touches and admires the cushions, pulls one into her lap. She looks out at the cityscape beyond the glass balcony doors, skittish. 'This is nice. I thought you had a house, though? I was surprised when the bus dropped me here.'

'I've tried to sell it but there's no takers. It's a bit of a shithole, you understand.'

She fusses with the tea things, waiting for more information but knowing not to push, Síon being momentarily out of her depths. She hunts for the chocolate chip cookies she never eats and finds them. Drops the packet. Twists her back as she squats to pick it up.

'Alright Róisín?' Síon knows about apprehension. Too many spirits crowding a person can do that. Rose thought she'd ended everything after Ireland but Síon is every bit the granddaughter of a púca and the sight is strong in her. She knows that was Rose's prelude to things yet to come.

Rose slides the tray onto the coffee table beside her computer, raking her fingers through her hair, uncommonly unruly and now very long, the wild red curls forming light-traps. 'Actually no. I'm quite manic. I've got my finals next week and life's been insane the last few months. Did you ever see Robin again?'

'Never again.'

'Doesn't matter. I'd have come to the funeral. Was there a funeral? Or did they burn— No, Sheldrú didn't have a vardo, did she? If someone had contacted me. And was there one for Billy? Is Gyofan alright? The family?'

'They're fine, and all. They didn't want you upset. Rose—?'

Rose saves her work on the laptop before closing it down. She is adamant she won't be distracted from this latest event, but it's not easy. She hugs a cushion to her own torso and turns her full attention to her visitor.

'So this? You live alone, like?' Síon takes up a mug of tea, adding copious spoons of sugar.

'Of course. Am I missing some innuendo?'

Síon tries to seem relaxed when she sees nothing but tragedy around her in the neatness. 'Of course? What's 'of course'?'

'Change of subject. Explain. How long are you here for?'

'Until after the graduation. Spring that is, Sheldrú said, so. Gyofan and the lads couldn't come but they wanted someone here.'

'I thought they didn't like me for leaving the way I did.'

'Why would you think that?' Síon reflects on all Rose's books, wondering how much it takes, in this way of life, to be a teacher of anything. 'I don't want to be interrupting, you know that?'

'Sweet Mother Mercy, it's not as if I don't need time off.' Rose catches herself using Robin's expression and remembers to breathe.

Síon, her legs curled up under her on the couch, pulls a letter from her pocket. 'Sheldrú said to give you this.'

Rose takes the letter from the envelope, unfolds it, noting the cramped style done in lead pencil. Not the work of anyone who's had much schooling. Then she admonishes herself for being elitist, her mind a roil of treacherous overgrown battlegrounds.

'Read it to me? I'm in the dark about a lot of what happened.'

Rose takes a while to study a little and so comprehend the forced English of it.

Darling Róisín, remember the time I asked if you loved anybody and I got a no? It's not the same now is it? I'm dead by the time you get this, but I have to tell a few importances. I've known the very best of it—and while it's grand to know love, it's also to be sure you'll know fear. When he looks at you with those eyes and you truly see him? Well you'll think, perhaps, he might be just like any other man, but he's not and never could be, so. Now some of the people call you an ice queen. No feeling for anyone or anything. They don't know what I know, what you, yourself, know. Robin is the best of them. Don't regret what happens. From Tír na n'Óg, Sheldrú.

Rose glances from the letter to Síon and back, confused about the Robin comments but refusing to go into it yet. 'I don't understand.'

'Finish it.' Síon's voice quiet, but slightly irritated by Rose's hesitancy and petulance. Rose refuses to be intimidated. It happens with the students of Síon's age all the time. Brazen girls who think anyone over twenty is useless unless they are a celebrity. She reads her sister wrong, though. The younger woman has inherited all the gifts Sheldrú said she would. She can read people like a true *drabarni*.

'You know what's in it?'

Síon shrugs. 'And read it out loud.'

'Why?'

'Magic. Some things are necessarily spoken, do I have to spell it out, *a cara*?'

Rose turns her mind back to the letter, immediately undone. She never saw this coming. '*P.S. He said to tell you this*: "*Who is this? And what is here? And in the lighted palace near died the sound of royal cheer; and they crossed themselves for fear, all the Knights at Camelot; but Lancelot mused a little space, he said, she has a lovely face. God in his mercy lend her grace, the Lady of Shalott.*"

'Robin called me that. Wait— No. He didn't. It's my memory playing tricks.' She can't seem to stop the tears from running out of her, untamed and sudden. 'I'm sorry.'

'Did he say he'd see you again?' Síon softens. She's found love with a one such as him, and now she, too, will never be the same. She can't say Sheldrú didn't warn her. She's here, a thousand miles away, but heard him from the airport to the bus, the crow on the frozen power lines, telling her how much he misses her already.

'Yes, but he didn't,' says Rose, keeping her voice from betraying her taking a mammoth effort. 'And what does she mean some of the people call me the ice queen?'

'The family never thought that. It's why Gyofan sent me. We love you, Róisín.'

Rose folds the letter and slides it back in the envelope, the slowness of the action giving her time to think. 'Tell you what. It's still early. You want to go get a dram? Great pub down the road.'

'I'm worn out, but I'm not dead. Are you joking?' Síon lights up, hugging Rose and grinning with mischief.

They cover up in warm things against the arctic night. Rose pulls on what she now thinks of as her faerie coat of many stories and doesn't bother tying her hair back. Síon is surprised. Is this the same Róisín?

. . .

PART 2

15

IN TWO PLACES AT ONCE

JOHN LANNARD leaves a request on Rose's voicemail asking her to give him a call. He'd like her to pop into the station when she can. He's been on the case of the murder ever since it happened and is surprised not to have heard from her, and that there's been a development.

Rose texts Lannard's cell phone number to let him know she'll be in sometime around nine in the morning and that her sister, Síon, insists on coming with her.

The two women pick up a take-away coffees downstairs at the police head-quarter's Jailhouse Rock cafe, then walk up the stairs to the first floor.

Lannard looks as though he's slept rough, out under a bridge or out all night on the job somewhere even dirtier than Lafayette Street, and his bulk stomps like an angry man from the door to the desk. Two laptops are open, and he looks from one to the other, flipping through paperwork layered in neat piles. A frown cuts deep lines between his eyebrows, resembling railroad tracks, that disappear up under his beanie. A uniformed cop is at another desk in the detective's office, typing up reports.

'Please come in,' he invites, sitting himself down and stretching his legs, taking up half the floor space. The women perch side by side on the forgettable couch that looks like it belongs in a dentist waiting room, not homicide investigation.

'John, this is Síon Borran, my friend from Ireland. You have something?'

He brings up a photo and ID page, and turns the screen to them. 'This guy, Billy Shando, was our best—our only witness. Not one other person from the pub that night has the same story. They all describe the antagonist differently. Drunks do my head in, Rose.'

'Billy Shando died,' says Síon.

There's a protracted silence as Lannard and the uniform cop exchange a look. Lannard's cell phone rings and he cuts it off.

'You want to tell me how come you know?' He sits with them, unscrewing the top off a bottle of soda water, 'because we haven't released that information yet.'

'His heart broke,' she advises. 'The priest found him in the chapel. We buried him in the graveyard there. No one had money to find his family.'

Lannard, his soda forgotten, pushes the beanie up off his forehead, to the hairline, in a gesture that indicates confusion. 'We're not talking about the same man.'

The moment is standoffish and uncomfortable, as though no one is speaking the same language. 'Billy Shando,' says Rose. 'From the pub.'

'Your father's best friend. Yes.' Lannard drinks from the bottle, his mind racing over how this doesn't add up. Almost trying to have the final say, that the case is closed.

'His what?' asks Rose.

Lannard leans his elbows on the table. 'What did Billy tell you if not about the connection with your father?'

'Not much at all until we traveled together.'

'We are definitely not talking about the same man.' Lannard leans back in his chair and gestures to the officer at the other desk in the room to join them because this is all too disjointed and incomprehensible.

'Billy Shando was scared out of his wits because of that night. He said the man who verbally abused your father was the devil. Here—'

He turns the file around and pushes it across the table to Rose. 'We were keeping him off the radar, in a safe house just in case, but he constantly took off. He's had an addiction to pain medication for years for the hip. As well as to the booze. The rubbish collectors found him the day before yesterday. Overdosed. Frozen solid down by the river.'

Síon's mind is working overtime attempting to make sense of the contradictory information. She knows it could be something to do with being in two places at once, but if that is the case—and Billy was powerful on the night of Ailín's departure ceremony, no doubt—then he knew more about the Fair Folk than he let on because this is their kind of doing.

No point suggesting anything like that to the Garda, she's not stupid, but this is getting silly. 'That couldn't be right.'

'John, he was in Ireland,' explains Rose. 'This is nuts. You're wrong.'

Lannard sighs, deciding. He shows her the autopsy report, including a photograph of the deceased Billy Shando.

'You going to tell me the truth about what's going on? Because I'm fucked if I know. The man we had in custody—Thomas Brodie Reed—the man Shando accused as being with the one doing all the talking, is also dead. We had him on priors and he was okay, but he upset someone in detention and was beaten to a pulp. Every one of his ribs piercing his lungs. He drowned in his own blood.

'Nobody says a thing and none of it makes sense, and yes I'm being as graphic as I can so you realize that perhaps this man had a grudge against your father. That perhaps Ailín Wen had enemies, after all, and that if you didn't even know he had a best friend perhaps your memory needs a serious jolting about other things you might not have considered. Because of what you have informed us concerning Ailín and your relationship.'

That shocks Rose. Has she been so bitter that her father could possibly have had a life beyond her idea of him, one that had nothing to do with the night? Was there more? King of the gypsies? A weak old drunk? He was only in his forties. If there was something else—he was a storyteller, after all—how much did her father make up so she wouldn't ask him who he really was? The realization that she really might not have known everything disturbing her deeply.

'I say this, because the assault wasn't a bit of fun, Ms. Wen. It has all the red flags of premeditated murder. No one randomly kills a useless, drunk, pathetic old man just to get his rocks off. Particularly when he was younger than me and none of his paper trails or official documents were real.

Rose's mouth hangs open. 'But, he got a social security check every fortnight.'

'You saw it?'

'No. He just always said.'

Lannard waits. Ever-patient.

'John, you are suggesting I didn't even know my own father. Now I don't know what to think. There must have been two Billy Shando's.' Rose allows Síon to take her hand, the look from the younger woman conveying, wordlessly, that anything is possible.

'Either that or one of us is crazy and I assure you it's not the Met Police. No offense meant, but—' He closes both the laptops, picks up the paperwork and hands it over to the uniform cop. Lannard shakes his head slowly, eyes downcast, defeated. 'We don't have a case now. That's it. I wanted to tell you in person. I'm leaving it open, and I'm not finished with this by a long-shot. It's just too much of a mystery to let die along with your father, but I can't see what else we can do for the moment. I'm sorry.'

Rose is like a deer in the headlights, disbelieving. Trying to process what she has been told altering her. What if everything she thought she knew about her life is false. She's just found out that who she is and where she's come from was never part of her relationship with her father. She remembers her mother's death only in dreams. So did it actually happen that way? Again, they never discussed Orla, and even the gypsies never alluded to her being murdered. Just that she died.

Why didn't she think to ask them more?

What the fuck is wrong with me? she wonders, the realization that she has lived in a world of her own making stark in her awareness. Perhaps none of it has been real. Bringing her to the brink of an anxiety attack.

John Lannard sighs. 'I'll make all the information available to you. You only have to put in a formal application, Ms. Wen.' He and the uniform officer leave Rose and Síon alone in the interview room.

...

16

THE HAUNT CAFE

IN THE COLDNESS OF EARLY WINTER, WHEN THE ICE is just an infant and the oak king does battle with the holly king, Rose and Síon are with Jeremy at the Haunt Cafe, the campus hangout to the college crowd.

Jeremy's been invited to give a lecture and demonstration—an extra curriculum class—on hacking and the WikiLeaks drama, for the remainder of the week. The women have filled him in on the strange police report situation and they are deep in forensics questioning, them both drinking coffee and Jeremy sipping a turmeric latte, oblivious to the other people. There's nothing to say that hasn't been said twice, three times over, none of it making any sense, and all three of them are introspective, even as Jeremy tries to work the situation out by getting them to backtrack. Over and over.

Rose filed the FOI request and it is being processed. She'd had no idea that her father's private papers were removed from the house when the police investigative team had gone through the place. She'd had no knowledge that a paper trail even existed, of who he was and what he did. She'd signed the release the day after Ailín's death, but that had slipped her mind completely. Because she hadn't cared. Angry. Distraught. His death had shocked her beyond belief. Her relief a stain of secret shame. When he was gone, she was conflicted. She had buried him and buried him and buried him, over and over in her dreams. She, she, she.

Robin had been right. Could she even love? Had she loved her father even as she convinced herself that she despised him? Her life is certainly never going to be the same knowing she knew nothing.

The dreams of her mother's murder were always so real but it had been reported that somebody else had killed Orla. Even though, yes, the hit had happened and so had the blood. The truth is that it had been her father accused and questioned. He had not been charged because even though the village woman, supposedly the only known witness, had sworn to him beating her it had been legally hearsay. She had described a dark, handsome tinker. And even if it had been one of them, the Travelers don't abide outsiders interfering in their ways. They have their own rules, their own laws. Even though a charge was laid against Ailín when the woman's priest had insisted, nothing had come of it. Funny that he had kept the paperwork though.

Had she really seen her mother's head hit the pavement? Was it true? Did she know? Did her dream remember it all wrong? Was her hatred of him justified? What kind of tricks does the mind play and who does the lying? Or was her father innocent? Was that man she remembers over and over, guilty, but protected? Or did the gypsies deal with her father and not a soul tell her a true and honest thing the entire time she was amongst them?

What are memories made of? Are they all just what we believe happened?

Sam sidesteps his way through the crowd before Rose notices him, having not seen him since the day of the funeral. Her arm is raised and he acknowledges her with a nod, pulling off his thick anorak, heading for the counter to order before joining them, taking his glasses from his pocket where he stowed them to keep them from freezing to his face outside.

'Hi Rose, I've missed you.' He kisses her on both cheeks and joins the group.

'Sam Black Squirrel, this is my sister of sorts, Síon Borran. Síon, Sam was my supervisor at the school where I did my internship. And my friend, of course. And Sam, Jeremy. We met on the plane and he's teaching me to be really bad at technology.'

Sam acknowledges Jeremy with a smile and a nod hello, before shaking hands with Síon.

'Sam Black Squirrel? What do you teach, then, Sam Black Squirrel?' She's already besotted.

He lets go grudgingly. He tries to be casual when he's not. Not at all. 'English literature. And poetry appreciation. Love. And writing techniques.'

'You a native with a name like that?'

Sam's eyes light first with laughter, then with attraction. 'Where in

Ireland are you from? I've got a thing for accents and you sound like a Dubliner? Or is it Connemara? I stayed a while, years ago. On a writer's retreat on Inishbofin. Do you know it? Near Dog's Bay, north of Galway. During one of your dreary excuses for winter.'

'I admit I've never known cold like this. I'd love to hear about the native spirit-world. You do have a spirit-world?'

'I don't believe I'm actually following this conversation,' laughs Jeremy, delighted.

'*Native* is politically offensive, I might add,' Sam adds, as charmingly as he is capable of being, 'but from you it's positively *Kerouac.*'

Jeremy and Rose raise mutual eyebrows thinking Síon has no idea what he means.

Jimmy and Emmet happen in at the same time, see the company, grab available chairs and crowd in at the table. Jeremy's eyes roam Jimmy like he's new world terrain to be explored.

'I'm James. Jimmy Wong.'

Jeremy introduces himself, stands and kisses Jimmy's cheeks, in the innocent European fashion, and Jimmy holds his palms beneath Jeremy's elbows, reciprocating.

'Who wants what?' Sam decides, standing and pulling his jeans up. *I should be putting body fat on, not dropping it*, he thinks, feeling a failure as an animal.

'I'll have what Jeremy's having,' says Jimmy, small change from his pockets dropping onto the table, frowning to make the task seem important.

'And I'll have a cappuccino thanks, princess,' Emmet chimes, a fool imitating a gay man.

Sam takes their money and steers a course effortlessly through the crowd to the counter.

'So Rosie, where you been?' Emmet has put on pounds while Rose was away. All around his middle. Rose, twisting the bangle at her wrist, like it is a talisman that can kill the man where he stands, wonders if he has Type Two diabetes yet. If it's the drink, like she's seen countless times before, the alcoholic doomed to a premature death.

'Traveling, Emmet. Studying.' To Síon, 'These people are also teachers where I did my training.'

'You graduated yet, Rosie-Rosie? You stood me up.'

'Not yet. You still a prick, Emmet?

Jimmy laughs at Emmet's shocked face and Jeremy, an audience, is amused.

Sam returns with the table number on a stand. 'What'd I miss?'

'Rose has explained Emmet for the new people,' advises Jimmy.

'In ten words or less?'

'Less.'

'And now, the introductions, ladies and gentlemen.' Sam sighs. 'Rose, correct me if I misinterpret, please, but Jimmy, this is Jeremy. And Emmet? This is Síon, and Síon I am Sam. Did I tell you that already?

'Síon,' Rose tells Jimmy, 'is from Ireland where I stayed.' Síon glances sideways at Rose from beneath hooded eyes that say more than words.

Sam is mesmerized. 'What am I missing, Rose?'

'Síon and I. We're family.'

'It's a great story, James,' Jeremy adds.

But Jimmy is confused. 'Hang on. What? You're not Irish, Rose.'

'Doesn't matter.' Does she really want to bother? After everything. All the questions? Justification? But Síon is having none of it.

'Just because a person's raised in another people's country doesn't make it their home. And we are gypsies, and proud of it, so.'

'You lost me. That's supposed to mean what?' Jimmy says, the staff person bringing their coffees and a pitcher of water, several glasses and a handful of hopeful menus.

'Tinkers and beggars,' smirks Emmet. 'Gypos, kid. Driving their trailer homes all over, doing bare-knuckle fighting and bullying the locals. I seen the docos.'

'Saw,' Rose growls, fire in her, after all. Everything rising towards the surface, itching for a fight. 'We're *anlucht siúil*. Look it up, dumb knuckle.'

Emmet, however, is standing like a joker on the stage. He's on a roll even when Sam sucks a breath between his teeth, cringing, thinking maybe he's got a spirit guide after all and that he ought to leave. 'Porn and bling and crime, Rosie-Rosie, and ice, in dirty concrete high rises. You're not one of them.'

Rose pushes her chair back from the table and pulls on her coat of many poems.

'Great look, Rose,' Jimmy smiles, surprisingly delighted. 'That's new for you.' Jeremy beams, whispering something in Jimmy's ear.

'We going, Síon?' Rose is as cold on the inside, now, as the day beyond the cafe heating.

Síon lifts her bag from the floor beside her chair, shouldering it.

'Rose? Oh god. We're so sorry,' Jimmy flusters.

'Leave me out of it, puppy,' laughs Emmet.

'*Dieu*,' whispers Sam, shrugging.

Rose squares up to Emmet and, to his startled surprise, chest-butts him.

'Don't *ever* call me Rosie again, trashbag. You have *never* earned that right.' And she, accompanied by Síon, strides off.

'Hang on, wait up!' calls Sam, as they walk towards the exit.

'*Trashbag?*' smirks Emmet to Jimmy Wong. 'And she's going to teach English and poetry to kids? Give them culture?'

Sam launches from his chair and follows the women outside. Jimmy and Jeremy adjust their seating to be closer to each other, while Emmet—the penny finally dropping—carries his cup to an empty table and turns his back, baffled.

The snow is heavier, as though the weather and Rose are in conspiracy, a realization of the mysteries of the world not lost on Síon, with visibility also down to a minimum. Rose has serious doubts about getting a cab home but traffic, although slow, is still obstinately moving.

Sam slips, rights himself, and walks as quickly as the ice-thick pavement allows, catching Síon by the sleeve.

'I'm really sorry about not understanding, *ma belle étranger*.' He is shy. Out of his depths a bit, but determined despite that, knowing he has finally met his muse. 'Síon, can we go out? Maybe see a film?'

'I'm staying with Rose.' Síon smiles at Rose, feigning naivety, but Rose has missed none of it. She bites off a glove, rummages in her bag, pulls out a small notebook and pen and writes. She tears out the page and hands it to Sam. 'My new number. Síon's got no phone. Yet.'

Sam takes it, satisfied.

Rose replaces her glove. 'What about those near-death experiences you once talked about, Sam? Remind me?'

'I'll call later, Síon,' he grins, his white teeth contrasting against the copper of his skin, his glasses already misting with the big freeze. 'And, yes, I've got a spirit-world.'

'Grand, ah, *étranger*,' smiles Síon, surprising him. Then she runs to catch up with Rose who's managed to wave down a cab.

Síon blacks the cell phone screen and returns the device to Rose who's curled up on the couch deep inside herself, trying to read but distracted. She's lost in thought about everything they and Jeremy discussed today. The implications John has exposed to her and her need to find the truth, no matter how devastating.

'He's coming by at six. Shite, but what'll I wear?

Rose gestures to her bedroom. 'Go through my stuff. Whatever you want.'

'You okay? You seem like your soul has deserted you.'

Rose closes her book and sits up with her hands between her knees. 'I've decided. I'm to sell the house. In the spring. I'm going there tonight to have a look at what need doing, maybe tidy up a bit. It's been closed up for a long time.

'Tonight? Not now Rose. Tomorrow. I can help.'

'Thanks. I mean it. But I'm pretty sure I need to do this on my own. Don't worry, I'll yell if I need a hand later. Knock yourself out tonight. Sam's pretty special, too. You get ready, I'll put the kettle on.'

Síon disappears into the bedroom, only to reappear moments later.

'Rose, I hate to tell you this but, by the faeries, your clothes are dead drab.'

'And you—*cailín*?' Rose retorts, alive for the first time in months. 'Is that it? Girl? *Cailín álainn*— See, I remembered—are the most gorgeous seventeen-year-old on the planet, so. Maybe we'll go shopping while you're here? Those tights and that little skirt and that hair of yours? You're going to kill Sam, seriously.'

Síon stops, considering, her face displaying a realization. 'Isn't tomorrow your birthday? The first official day of winter that some eejit forgot to tell the weather gods?'

Rose ignores her, the fact irrelevant.

…

17

SAYETH THE RAVEN

'*SO, IT COMES TO THIS,* SAYS ROBIN from somewhere beyond the known world of space and time, that *Once upon a midnight dreary, while I pondered, weak and weary, over many a quaint and curious volume of forgotten lore—*

The taxi pulls up at 64 Lafayette Street New Rathmore West. The snowstorm has stopped. The night is sentinel silent.

'*…while I nodded, nearly napping, suddenly there came a tapping—*

She pulls hard on the gate to dislodge the snow piled up against it, before making her way to the front door without once slipping on the dirty black, acidic ice.

'*As of someone gently rapping—*

She sighs.

'*rapping at my chamber door. 'Tis some visitor, I muttered—*

Rose steps, cautious of her mindset, to the dark and lonely house, the only illumination coming from the harshness of the streetlights. She closes the front door quietly behind her and stands with her back against it.

'tapping at my chamber door. Only this, and nothing more. Ah, distinctly I remember, it was in the bleak December—

She switches on the light, but the bulb blows with a fizz of sparks.

'Typical,' she sighs, padding silently across the thin carpet of the freezing living room, the smell of mouse droppings and urine overwhelming, making her gag. She turns the knob to go into her old room and almost changes her mind. There isn't a reason, is there?

She moves down the hall to her father's room, where the door is wide open, just as she'd left it. She steps across the threshold and stands statue-still, trying to get her bearings, being in here only ever once.

At his bed, scattered with musty, dirty coverings, her night vision slowly adjusts to recognize individual articles of information. She registers that there are no monsters, then fixates on Ailín's forsaken dressing gown. And remembers.

Ailín is in his twenties, the most handsome man she ever saw, walking beside the family's vardo. Him smiling, holding the bridles of their piebald vanners.

Ailín and Orla dancing near an open hearth fire, musicians playing a lively jig, but them in a world of love, slow-moving to a sound that only they can hear.

Herself playing with other children, covertly watching how her parents love each other with their eyes, as they go about their day within the camp.

Hiding under the covers of her little bed when he came in drunk and fell over things. Them screaming at each other, him in a rage of jealousy that happened every time, the accusations unbearable and insane. Later guilt-ridden because he'd accidently smashed the mother-of-pearl-inlaid rosewood box containing her *seanmáthair's*—grandmother's—sorceries. The dark blue velvet pouch of magic she'd stolen. The small horse brasses, collection of tiny painted bird bones that she once used to tell fortunes and the bewitched, pale holey stones gathered from the shorelines of windswept beaches she had been compelled to wander when she could, all of which had been her gift—her legacy—to Orla on the day she wedded Ailín. No one ever guessed that Rose had collected them all and made for them a pouch of that indigo velvet, hidden amongst her belongings.

The violent crack as her mother's head hits the concrete sidewalk and the slow pooling of blood, her eyes wide open staring at the sky. In town?

Ailín on his knees, weeping as the caravan burns. Later, dirty and sweaty, older and worn and never smiling as he works in his garden.

In his chair in the sitting room, leaning towards Rose, a look of mischief on his face, his lips turning up, she thinks, she thinks. Him saying *Róisín! Are you listening?* Drunk as a botched suicide.

Rose picks up the dressing gown and presses it to her face, breathing deeply. Robin's voice in her head saying, 'Did you not love him a little though?' and her answering, 'No. He was pathetic.'

Dad, for god's sake, you have no idea how much I loved you.

She is buried under the grief of all the unsaid, her sobs harsh and deep down, crueler than she knew possible until, her ribs ache and her throat is raw; she can hardly take a breath.

Like a sleepwalker she returns to her room, wrapped in the smell of him, and for the first time in her adult life she pulls the worn blue pouch containing her grandmother's treasures and clutches it to herself, resigned to never abandoning it again but, even now, almost afraid to take its contents from their hiding place just in case her father's ghost is stirred with the knowledge of what she thinks she stole all those years ago. Defiant, for all that. Brave. Claiming it as her own, her birthright, as seems fitting on a night such as this. A night of what she thinks of as an ending, oblivious to future ramifications.

She staggers back to his bed and wraps the scent-of-him-dressing gown around herself, curling amongst the stained pillows under the thrift shop eiderdown like a hedgehog protecting its vulnerable belly, exhausted, puffy and snotty, wiping her nose on her sleeve, the thought occurring fleetingly that without the warmth of a fire she could freeze to death tonight.

Hours later and a faint, odd sound wakes her. Someone whistling a tune that's almost familiar. She's disoriented, attempts to stand, her grandmother's bundle still clutched in her hand, but sitting back down on the bed until the room makes sense.

The tune catches on the air of night for a few seconds more, then switches off.

Rose can't leave it alone. She hunts for the sound through the dark and memory-laden house. You know how you listen? Sure it's there? Tilting one ear up, then the other? She tries the light switch in the kitchen pointlessly, eventually opening the back door... And staring, disbelieving. The little back garden is blanketed in snow but is kaleidoscopic with flowers, mostly roses gone feral.

She's sure she can hear him. The shovel. The grunt. If she's gone mad, so be it. If she's dies of hypothermia, then she's okay with that. If this is normal. How mind-altering if it's magic. The impossibility of this being real. That it's real. That she doesn't know what is real from what's not, or isn't supposed to be, or is and isn't agreed to. There probably never will be answers.

Then the snowstorm begins again with a howl of blinding majesty, only lasting half an hour before becoming a silent fall of whiteness.

Though it doesn't really protect her from the elements Rose wraps the dressing gown more tightly around herself and closes the door. Thinking she might be alive, after all.

Robin drops from the branches of that big old skeletal rowan tree. Into a crouch. He stands and dusts himself off, pulling his battered top hat further over his ears until almost comedic, his gold earrings glinting in the haloed light coming off the streetlamps and mindless of the snow damping on his shaggy hair and his shabby clothing. Instead he raises his face to the wonder of winter, in faerie ecstasy.

At a bush of blood red, full-blown roses he plucks one, unaffected by the piercing of many thorns. Then he pads around the side of the house to the porch facing Lafayette Street, using the front way in so as not to frighten her, and he rat-a-tat-tats on the door, waiting. Knowing she must hide Róisín Séala's secret pouch—her grandmother's magic— before she will open up to him.

...

18

TINKLE, TINKLE

ROSE HOSTS A HUMBLE BOOK LAUNCH for *Under Snow, Poems and Other Wanderings*, down on the south side by the old docks, on the almost forgotten, undeveloped part of the city. Copperhead Lane. Dimity's Books and Cafe. Downstairs in the basement with its old tables and long-dead taxidermied animals and birds, books stacked to the ceiling and undressed stone walls, lit by candles and small lamps, with mismatched, overstuffed chairs. A place loved by the few that know of it.

Jeremy has come with Jimmy, dressed for an occasion much more imposing, and proud to have done so. Síon is wrapped in Sam's arms.

They now live together with Janet. All listen to the last of Rose's reading from the back of the slim volume. The others there are the wild people, the ghosts, the poets, the sinners, the lost visionaries and dreamers, hidden from the spotlight of the world, and some, more likely here for the warmth rather than any book. And the gypsies, of course.

Rose doesn't care. Robin sits on his stool, beside her, a beaded and bangled arm draped around her shoulders, just a shabby young man in jeans, and a grey hoodie under a sparrow-brown waistcoat, his flattened-out old top hat, currently adorned with raven and cockerel feathers bunched in the ribbon, placed on the table beside her stack of copies. He has his fob chain attached to a button and draped, like a secret, in his waistcoat pocket. He pulls out the worn and tarnished silver watch and clicks it open, more as reassurance that the thing is still broken, the hands not having moved for over a hundred years. It makes him smile. The inside is inscribed with *NEVERMORE* followed by a question mark. Then he tucks it away again.

The non-descript man, with the pale red hair, in black jeans, a black shirt and a black jacket, wearing soft kid gloves and a smile for Rose, nods at Robin as he hands her his copy of her book to sign.

She holds her pen, poised, tilting her head in a gesture asking for what he wants as a dedication.

'To my granddaughter,' he says, with a slight accent she can't quite place.

'You're not old—' She doesn't complete the sentence because of a certain, dangerous, unreadable look in his eyes. 'That's all?'

'That'll do for now,' he answers from that forgettable face.

At the counter upstairs he asks Merrin, long black hair, red lips, silver pentagram worn defiantly about her neck, a diamond, embedded into a front tooth, exposed by her bright and candid for-the-customer smile, to please make sure Rose gets this copy before she goes home, and Merrin agrees.

'Do I know you?' she asks. But he pulls the door open to the relentless inane tinkle of yet another overhead bell without answering.

Deep in the silent, still-icy night it is the witching hour and the miniscule, almost imperceptible lumps on the branches of every seeming-dead tree in the city, crack open a little with the promise of spring beyond the perpetual freeze.

The bus pulls into the empty terminal on its last run and the man in black, Leoghaire ó naSìogaì, being his true name, named for the fox in his blood, gets off. He climbs ancient steps, hewn from the solid rock, once part of the mountain chain, sagging in the middle now, from the countless feet that trod them back when the steel foundry was at its heyday and people had employment. Not like now. Automation killed that. Yes, a few old, tired workers, who don't know what else to do, will climb these same stairs in the morning before daylight, to fulfill meaningless jobs.

Their hearts will keep beating long enough to get back home in the night, it being winter and light failing at four o'clock in the afternoon as it does. To feed the kids, have a spliff, drink one too many beers and think it'll be okay, pop a couple of Valium and switch on YouTube.

The man with the soft mouth and the strong features, that can also be unnoticed if he chooses, removes his gloves and shoves them in the back pocket of his black jeans mindlessly, like he's done a thousand times before, revealing a bluebird tattoo on one hand and a broken chalice on the other, He pads, as quiet as that fox, along Lafayette Street. Past the kebab joint, and the Sizzlers, empty, except for the two uniform cops, Kevlar vests, shiny black boots and cool navy blue uniforms, guns and handcuffs at their belts, cams and coms on their helmets and shoulders, stopping on their way to the highway for burgers and Red Bull.

The young man in the silly uniform is still behind the counter of the 7-Eleven, selling fags and porn magazines and wishing for the colors of Mumbai.

He passes the junked cars up on bricks, well-stacked by practiced hands, and one rundown clapboard house after the other, the gardens long gone to seed and cooch grass. He slows, for just a minute, at 64 Lafayette Street, and dips his head in homage to the rowan.

'Hello tree,' he whispers to her, all skeletal and hopeful.

He sings low in his throat as he passes it, letting it all go. '*Through these fields of destruction, baptisms of fire. I've witnessed your suffering, as the battle raged higher and though they did hurt me so bad, In the fear and alarm, you did not desert me, da-dum-diddydum.*' He whistles the chorus as he lifts the collar of his black *s*hirt before pulling the narrow, stiff white strip from his pocket and grunting, with a strange aching effort for such a seemingly fit, seemingly young man. He clips it behind his neck, fingers the rebellious lock of hair that somehow always gets raggedy and flyaway, no matter how much money he spends on bespoke barbers and extracts a worn burnished rosary from inside his jacket, wrapping its familiarity around a hand.

At the end of Lafayette Street, taking up the whole of a piece of land claimed by the church over two hundred years ago, is a building of cut rock with stained glass windows, also barred because if anything gets broken into in this neighborhood it's not going to be this, its heavy, tamper-proof oak doors held in place by stained steel brackets.

Nearby is the little private rectory, a garden almost buried beneath the meter of snow, the canes of ancient roses protruding like a dead man's fingers clawing uselessly at his coffin lid, covered in thorns and pulled tight against wooden stakes begging, *please let us be all brambly and wild this spring*. 'Sorry,' he whispers.

As abruptly as his acknowledgement he forgets them and what he has said. Seconds pass into eternity. He slots the old iron key into the big antiquated lock and turns it, releasing the mechanism, before clicking the Bluetooth *CrimSafe* security code into his phone, the door opening like the purr of a kitten in the silence of the icy night.

'Make it easier for me next time, you Halfling. Calling yourself Robin all hoity-toity-like. What is it this time? Redbreast? Hood? Goodfellow? Ah yes, Kipling—because, *deartháir*, I'm getting too positively ancient for this, so.'

He whispers quiet and low, smiling like only those of great age do. 'And let her go now. I know you have planted her, and that a new story quickens in her already. Don't you fuck this up.'

'And by the way, Monsieur Marius,' he hears in the frost of the cold dark night, *'I believe that I was a little bit in love with you.'*

'Feck off with Les Misérables, you deadly old *rómánsúil* púca.' And he shakes his head, chuckling softly as he pulls the door shut, no one to see what happens next. The seeming young man, behind this wall of christendom, suddenly fades of color, greys, wrinkles, loses form and shrinks, discorporating and becoming soil.

The old priest, whose body the faerie has inhabited, withers into death, but he is smiling as he remembers where he's been and who he's loved and been loved by, and what a sham this religion really is, when the story of Oisín, son of Finn McCool, in Tír na n'Óg for all these mortal years, is who he really is. And it calls him back. Him knowing he never should have thrown his legs over the back of that white horse that Ailín Wen had named Manannán Mac Lír, and that all he wants, as he turns to dust, is to lie in Niamh's arms forever. To taste the silver apples of the moon and the golden apples of the sun.

Before dawn the John Lannard lookalike, whose real name is not to be spoken but who never was what he called himself, playing his part for as long as he did, quietly closes the police-issue vehicle door and pulls the beanie away from his long, dreadlocked hair. The air momentarily flutters with the flyaway blackbird feathers and those of doves and starlings that escape as the hat is removed. He breathes the clean brightness of the icy night before walking to the chapel door and willing it to open. His work will be done after disappearing the priest's shell and sending his shade to whatever the man thought of as the afterlife. He's not sorry. Faeries don't consider *sorry* appropriate.

Happy birthday, to you, he whispers, only loud enough for any passing hound to hear, *happy birthday to you. Happy birthday dear Róisín, happy birthday to you.*

Across town, on waking, the real John Lannard weeps as the dream dissolves, leaving facing his life, lonelier and more crushing than ever. He wishes his wife would come back to him, unaware that she has decided she loves him after all and has packed to come home.

...

PART 3

19

THE STORYTELLER'S SECOND INTERRUPTION

WHEN WE'RE ANONYMOUS AND LOST, SAYS Sheldrú, *all dead and all, we have to invent ourselves, methinks. When we've not got a mirror, nor no ancient story to hear that we just* know *is true. When we cause trouble, when we don't do what society thinks is normal, when we don't behave in an approved way, we're going to get a hiding or a slayer of a dressing down, that's sure. Somebody's going to want to shut us under the stairs, that's sure. Be warned. Me and you might be thought of as ornery, or pig-headed or even somewhat arrogant. Foolery. Or* a piece of work *(whatever that means). But what about when that's an insult because it's untrue, and others choose to see the world through eyes not those of the likes of us?*

One way of living with being anonymous and lost happens when there's nobody to offer us stories with life in them. To become sullen. Resentful. Maybe you work like crazy to fit in. I understand that. Loneliness is a way, so. But I must say that even though this is a track through the forest that myth suggests drives a body mad, it is not the path only trodden deep by deer, but by wolves hunting *deer. Because there comes a time when the pretending to be what you're not is like an old, sad pelt hanging on the back of the kitchen door that used to belong to a selkie who died without it in the long ago. It smells of rot. And that's what'll happen to the person gets too scared to be their true self.*

Stories instantaneously bypass the ego. The ego cannot absorb the entire pith of story. The story as a form of entertainment. While the ego is kept happy, thinking it is being entertained, the soul and the spirit are listening deeply. The flow of images in stories is medicine—similar medicine to listening to the ocean or gazing at sunrises. No direct interaction has occurred—the ocean did not jump into your body and fill you. But there is something about seeing, hearing, and smelling the ocean that has bypassed the ego, and straightened out many things that were in disarray within the psyche.

Dr. Clarissa Pinkola Estes

Regarding the ego, I disagree. It's making up our own minds that's significant, so. The other thing what makes sense, is being in your own mind and self by learning. Now, that can be a labyrinthine, maze-like piece a work, because not all information that passes itself off as knowledge, is knowledge, you understand. Much of it was copied from the notes of another student who maybe didn't have the right answers either. Cheating when the exam was on, for nothing. And there's me thinking that I must have snuck the right answers because I didn't understand that what I was copying was wrong.

Despite the deceptions I know many, many gatherers nowadays. Some are scholars and teachers, sure as day follows night, but the best among them are the storytellers, questioners and hunters. Modern interpreters of myth and legend. Challengers of Valhalla, so to speak.

The center of any maze is what happens if we get there. It's the discovery that hidden within all we learn just might be a nugget of gold. An unborn child. A puppy still unlicked in the caul. An egg nestled deep within lore.

There it is then. There's no way to deal with this world as a person. People have been too often, and untruthfully, too much at the center and not looking for the story, just trying to plant what someone else said, like hippies with crystals at Stonehenge. Sure it is, they mean well, but it's a bit oopsie, truth be told.

Myth is a story without an author, did you know that? Passed through the generations like a rose on a vine. And myth is also the soil in which the vine gains soul. Deep rootedness. From which all of us, who walk that edge and beg that cloud to rain on this desert of shallow verbiage, unfurls from seed to stem to root to bud to leaf to fruit.

I have been as much a pigeon and the north wind as I have been a cinderblock tenement and an orphanage of abandonment. You too, huh?

There are ropes around our wildness, so. Some are rough and cruel, yes, but some are silky and seemingly-languid, and they're as intentional as chain.

The Anglo-Saxons had a word, *geidd*, to describe the intensities and beauties of language at its most transcendental, regardless of whether it was found in speech or on paper, in a fireside ballad or an epic saga recited in the longhouse. It was what they regarded as the true poetic spirit. The giedd is the delicious scent that Trickster seeks in this confluence of influence.

Martin Shaw, A Branch from the Lightning Tree.

It is unwise to trust the way history is written, just a warning, maybe? Or even what we've told ourselves to believe is our own story. Challenge it, I suggest. Ask who wrote it or who else remembers it; because it is truly being lifted up every day, from the land of dreams, anew and endless with potential.

Consider whether the rememberers might been biased. I mean, what eejit invented the lie that Mórrigan *is a battle goddess—a battle queen—when the one word is two words? And* queen *is not an Irish word? So, what're we talking about here? And was there war in Ireland except in the stories? Course, it was never written as war, and did anybody count the dead before the famine? And if that landscape was represented by a person or a clan why did they fight? Who perpetuates the idea of warfare on another people when that's the language of empires, rape and broken treaties? When did sovereignty become human in difference to horse and faeries and púca and selkies and talking ravens?*

Shall we, then, accept the dabbler-verbiage and kiddie-pool-thinking of people adding the same diatribe, and hot piss in their bathers, in the ocean, in secret? Or can we bypass all that and seek good honest dirt. Humus.

We have to be tough-hided, though, and walk with our scent-sense in prime function. Earth has taken a rather preposterously long time to create the depth in which deep ancestral roots thrive. If, in stupidity, we seek only to please ourselves and not be the landscape and the puppies, badgers, owlets, hares, kittens, salmon, turtles, warblers, bears, mackerel and wolves, starlings, worms, dragons and gorillas, and, oh, every other species who are also *the landscape we will have entered the illusion of a person-made fairyland that has no validity in deep-forest-dreams and wandering. We will have drunk the poison and eaten the lollies and taken the pyrite. Of pretenders and fools, only to find it dust when we awaken.*

The relationship between thinking and walking is also grained deep into the language history, illuminated by perhaps the most wonderful etymology I know. The trail begins with our verb to learn, meaning to 'acquire knowledge'. Moving backwards in language time, we read the Old English *leornian*, 'to get knowledge', to be cultivated.' From *leornian* the path leads us further back, into the fricative thickets of Proto-Germanic, and to the word *liznojan*, which has a base sense of 'to follow or to find a track' (from the Proto-Indo-European prefix leis-, meaning 'track'). 'To learn' therefore means at root—at route—'to follow a track'. Who knew? Not I, and I am grateful for the etymologist-explorers who uncovered those lost trails connecting 'learning' with 'path-following.

Robert Macfarlane, The Old Ways.

…

SERENITY DE ANGELES

Artist, photographer and poet.

And the fire from his throat has captivated all the broken,
With the dreams and spells and silence that his lyrics leave unspoken,
And with the lickings of guitar that seal the secrets of his song,
He lulls the crowd into a home in which, though broken, they belong.

In a small cottage perched in the clouds of Blackheath, in the Blue Mountains west of Sydney, Australia, a thousand feet above the valley below, Serenity was born with that caul, supposed to prevent a ship from sinking in some wild storm on the high seas, and she was warned never look down. But. Of course, who listens to warnings?

LY DE ANGELES

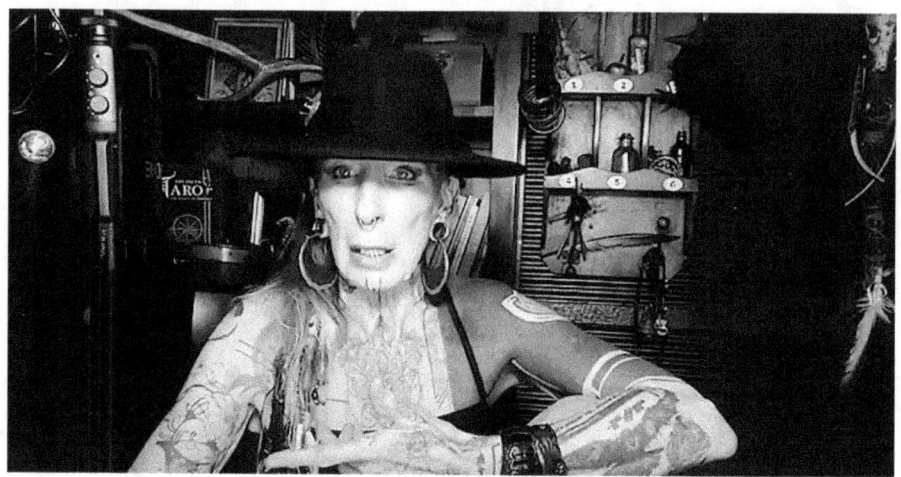

In print since 1987, firstly through Unity/Prism, Dorset, England, Ly de Angeles (true name, Lore de Angeles Whitehorse) is a, scholar, deep ecologist, mythographer and master storyteller. She also has the *sight*. She has three living children.

My preferred writing style is magical realism. Because realism is over-rated and usually by someone claiming an authority biased by Medieval monks, and an opinion that just makes me sigh. Again.

WEBSITE loredeangeles.com

OTHER BOOKS BY LY DE ANGELES

The Way of the Goddess, Unity/Prism, England, 1987

The Way of Merlyn, Unity/Prism, England, 1990

Witchcraft Theory and Practice, Llewellyn, USA, 2000

When I See the Wild God, Llewellyn, USA, 2002

Pagan Visions for a Sustainable Future, Llewellyn, USA, 2004

The Quickening, 1st in the Traveler Series, Llewellyn, USA, 2005

The Shining Isle, 2nd in the Traveler Series, Llewellyn, USA, 2006

Tarot Theory and Practice, Llewellyn, USA, 2007

Magdalene, Witch of the Grail Legends, 2012

The Feast of Flesh and Spirit, poetry and reflections, 2013

Priteni, the Decimation of the Indigenous Britons, 2015

Initiation, A Memoir, 2016

The Skellig, a Shapechanger Epic, 2017

Witch, For Those Who Are, 2018

Under Snow, 3rd in the Traveler Series, 2019

Advanced Tarot, 2020

Brave | For the Unclaimed People, 2021

Crow Magic, A Novella, 2022

The Changeling, From Winter Spring is Born, 4th in the Traveler Series, 2022

ACKNOWLEDGEMENTS

Thanks, Lynn Parlett, for your 2024, proof read. Thank you for graciously finding those gnarly, unrealized typos. To Stacey Ingram out woop-woop, or, rather, Nichols Rivulet, for the studio space to record the audiobook as well as the deep chat and mutual respect.

Hi, Sheana Keene of BlueGrace Music. Wherever you are now I wish you fascination. Thank you for the mistake at the book launch tour for The Quickening of 2006. For sending me on a chase of wild geese, in Co Cork, that landed me with Bev and Del, *anlucht súile*, instead. For the hospitality of those government-legislated sedentary Irish Travelers who took me to the real Castle Pook and told me the legend of William Shakespeare; of how he was inspired to write Midsummer Night's Dream.

Big hello to the street-wise poets of Galway who scared me almost to death before plying me with coffee, at Tigh Neachtain, for the stories of my tattoos.

To the family, never met, who found us, (so, I suppose, to ancestry.com). Travelers also, Romanichal, revitalizing our heritage and prompting a name change when honestly and finally being claimed.

Such a relief to know it was all true, after all.

NEW RELEASE 2022
Book 4 in the Traveler Series
ISBN 979-8834120735

THE CHANGELING

WINTER BECOMING SPRING

Genre: *Magical Realism*

Set after the food riots of 2025, *The Changeling* is a faerie story. But not for children. Not pretty. It is ecological. Breaks the rules. While remaining true to environmentalism and seasonal legend, *The Changeling* confuses and disturbs. The author explains, at the end of the book, as she does so here, how these stories originally came about. They were published in *When I See the Wild God* (USA, 2004) which was followed by three books of the same genre as the short stories. The reason for *The Changeling* is ecological, animist, and psychological and a book intended as an enchantment.

MERCY RILEY was born up the road from the village of Weary Bay. Under the indifferent eyes of eight nuns at Our Lady of Perpetual Sorrows Mother and Baby Home. A place of shame. An institution of secrets. Never permitted to know her mother; Mercy is a name invented by strangers. While social acceptability is not her destiny, neither is obscurity. At age of thirteen, she escapes.

She is discovered and aided by Black Annis, the punkish, crow-like sídhe woman. Taken in by Annis' clan, the Travelers, she is housed with Maisie Raith, Weary Bay's generations-deep practitioner of witchcraft and healing, from whom she learns some semblance of what it means to live beyond a walled, barred institution. She is taught to foretell a person's death through tarot cards, but she is also educated, maybe randomly, maybe by design, to kill with precision.

MORCANT intends to be the destroyer of words. Deluded into believing he is of the unseelie court, he is tech-savvy and cruel. Someone named Raven has written the code to exquisite music. He must possess him at any cost, including brutalizing one of his own; a random factor named the Artful Dodger, who is also not what he seems.

RAVEN is a wild, dark faerie man, an unfortunate empath, reclusive, busted, dangerous, and lost. Hospitalized for fighting. Spent time in prison. He has learned the art of computer code and has created music not heard in the world in living memory. He must remember his *shine*, for long enough, to deliver his music to the Great Mystery. He does not realize his love for Mercy is skewed. He understands only when the work of magic is done.

HENRY WABAUN is a cop—a detective of indigenous heritage—investigating a murder during the riot. He is assigned to interview Raven, as a witness, but that is not what happens. Raven draws the policeman into the web of strange occurrences. He has a purpose.

SPARROW, stick-thin and odd, merely tries to stay alive. To hide from the *slúag*. Also from the Mother and Baby Home, she is an artist who, also, is not what she seems. She draws victim and murderer. It is her work that moves the chess pieces upon the board. She thinks maybe DÉJÀVU DELACROIX is her friend when nothing could be further from the truth.

HUNTER, not a person, but a first forest. Guardian of the Great Mystery, or the other way around, who cannot interfere in human affairs so works with the fáidh and other manifestations of wilderness and environment, to keep the world alive.

THE CHANGELING is not who anyone thinks, and neither is anyone else.